COSMIC LAUGHTER

COSMIC LAUGHTER

SCIENCE FICTION
FOR THE FUN OF IT

compiled by

joe haldeman

holt, rinehart and winston

NEW YORK   CHICAGO   SAN FRANCISCO

ACKNOWLEDGMENTS

"A Slight Miscalculation" by Ben Bova. Copyright © 1971 by *The Magazine of Fantasy and Science Fiction*. Reprinted by permission of the author.

" 'It's a Bird! It's a Plane!' " by Norman Spinrad. Copyright © 1970 by Norman Spinrad, first published in *Gent.*, 1967.

"The Robots Are Here" by Terry Carr. Copyright © 1967 by Galaxy Publishing Corporation, first published in *If*, May, 1967.

"I of Newton" by Joe Haldeman. Copyright © 1970 by Ultimate Publishing Co., Inc. Reprinted by permission of the author.

"The Men Who Murdered Mohammed" by Alfred Bester. Copyright © 1957 by Alfred Bester, first published in *The Best of Fantasy and Science Fiction*, Doubleday & Company, Inc., Garden City, 1957.

"To Serve Man" by Damon Knight. Copyright 1950 by Galaxy Publishing Corporation, first published in *Galaxy*.

"The Bomb in the Bathtub" by Thomas N. Scortia. Copyright © 1972 by Thomas N. Scortia, first published in *Galaxy Science Fiction*, February, 1957.

"Gallegher Plus" by Henry Kuttner. Copyright 1952 by Henry Kuttner, reprinted by permission of Harold Matson Company, Inc.

Library of Congress Cataloging in Publication Data

Haldeman, Joe W   comp.
    Cosmic laughter.
    CONTENTS: Bova, B. A slight miscalculation.—
Spinrad, N. It's a bird, it's a plane!—Carr, T.
The robots are here. [etc.]
    1. Science fiction. [1. Science fiction]
I. Title.
PZ5.H13Co   [Fic]   72–91652
ISBN 0–03–006931–9

Printed in the United States of America
Designed by Jack Ellis for Anthony Paccione Associates
First edition

For Mother and Dad

INTRODUCTION

A LOT OF SCIENCE FICTION IS DEADLY SERIOUS. Authors spin cautionary tales telling us how we are "Doing Ourselves In." They invent whole new universes, new races of men, as settings and casts for vast dramas. With all of the Universe, past, present and future, for a canvas, it is little wonder that the brush is usually broad and the strokes bold.

Science fiction makes a lot of noise; rayguns zapping, planets colliding, cosmic metaphors rumbling. But if you listen closely, you'll hear an occasional chuckle, a belly-laugh, even, and over there—just four light years southeast of Alpha Centaurus—a chorus of raucous laughter. Because you can also have science fiction just for the fun of it.

The only thing the following stories all have in common is that they made me laugh. Otherwise, it's a very mixed bag. You'll find constant slapstick wackiness in Henry Kuttner's fabulous machines, but also a Damon Knight story that seems very sober and serious—until the very last line. We have the blackest of black humor and some purely enjoyable froth. Both in the same story, as a matter of fact, by a strange lowercase person called andy offutt.

You're about to meet such improbable people as Caedman Wickes (Private Investigator, Specializing in Odd Complaints), an army of Clark Kents, one Dr. Moneygrinder, and Felix Funck, Supershrink. There are a few absentminded professors, naturally, and even one who becomes progressively absent-bodied.

And the machines: a huge apparatus apparently constructed only to eat dirt while singing "St. James Infirmary," a tin beach ball with Old World charm, a transparent robot in love with its own innards, and an egotistical H-bomb that talks and has one blue eye.

But all is not frivolity and lightheartedness, oh no. These stories deal with such mighty serious topics as catastrophic earthquakes, a world gone insane, anthropophagy, the Spider Invasion, and a device made to blow up the whole Universe for, uh, therapy.

The topics, at least, are serious.

Joe Haldeman
Florida, 1973

CONTENTS

COSMIC
LAUGHTER

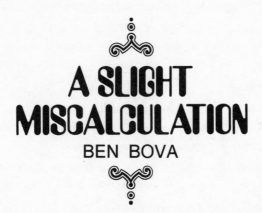

A SLIGHT MISCALCULATION

BEN BOVA

NATHAN FRENCH WAS A PURE MATHEMATICIAN. HE worked for a research laboratory perched on a California hill that overlooked the Pacific surf, but his office had no windows. When his laboratory earned its income by doing research on nuclear bombs, Nathan doodled out equations for placing men on the Moon with a minimum expenditure of rocket fuel. When his lab landed a fat contract for developing a lunar flight profile, Nathan began worrying about air pollution.

Nathan didn't look much like a mathematician. He was tall and gangly, liked to play handball, spoke with a slight lisp when he got excited, and had a face that definitely reminded you of a horse. Which helped him to remain pure in things other than mathematics. The only possible clue to his work was that, lately, he had started to squint a lot. But he didn't look the slightest bit nervous or high-strung, and he still often smiled his great big toothy, horsy smile.

When the lab landed its first contract (from the State of California) to study air pollution, Nathan's pure thoughts turned—naturally—elsewhere.

"I think it might be possible to work out a method of predicting earthquakes," Nathan told the laboratory chief, kindly old Dr. Moneygrinder.

Moneygrinder peered at Nathan over his half-lensed bifocals. "Okay, Nathan, my boy," he said heartily. "Go ahead and try it. You know I'm always interested in furthering man's understanding of his universe."

When Nathan left the chief's sumptuous office, Moneygrinder hauled his paunchy little body out of its plush desk chair and went to the window. *His* office had windows on two walls: one set overlooked the beautiful Pacific; the other looked down on the parking lot, so that the chief could check on who got to work at what time.

And behind that parking lot, which was half filled with aging cars (business had been deteriorating for several years), back among the eucalyptus trees and paint-freshened grass, was a remarkably straight little ridge of ground, no more than four feet high. It ran like an elongated step behind the whole length of the laboratory and out past the abandoned pink stucco church on the crest of the hill. A little ridge of grass-covered earth that was called the San Andreas Fault.

Moneygrinder often stared at the fault from his window, rehearsing in his mind exactly what to do when the ground started to tremble. He wasn't afraid, merely. careful. Once a tremor had hit in the middle of a staff meeting. Moneygrinder was out the window, across the parking lot, and on the far side of the fault (the eastern, or "safe," side) before men half his age had gotten out of their chairs. The staff talked for months about the astonishing agility of the fat little waddler.

A year, almost to the day, later the parking lot was slightly fuller, and a few of the cars were new. The pollution business was starting to pick up, since the disastrous smog in San Clemente. And the laboratory had also managed to land a few quiet little Air Force contracts—for six times the amount of money it got from the pollution work.

Moneygrinder was leaning back in the plush desk chair, trying to look both interested and noncommittal at the same time, which was difficult to do, because he never could follow Nathan when the mathematician was trying to explain his work.

"Then it's a thimple matter of transposing the progression," Nathan was lisping, talking too fast because he was excited as he scribbled equations on the fuchsia-colored chalkboard with nerve-rippling squeaks of the yellow chalk.

"You thee?" Nathan said at last, standing beside the chalkboard. It was totally covered with his barely legible numbers and symbols. A pall of yellow chalk dust hovered about him.

"Um. . . ." said Moneygrinder. "Your conclusion, then. . . ."

"It's perfectly clear," Nathan said. "If you have any reasonable data base at all, you can not only predict when an earthquake will hit and where, but you can altho predict its intensity."

Moneygrinder's eyes narrowed. "You're sure?"

"I've gone over it with the Cal Tech geophysicists. They agree with the theory."

"H'mm." Moneygrinder tapped his desk top with his pudgy fingers. "I know this is a little outside your area of interest, Nathan, but . . . ah, can you really predict actual earthquakes? Or is this all theoretical?"

"Sure you can predict earthquakes," Nathan said, grinning like Francis the movie star. "Like next Thursday's."

"Next Thursday's?"

"Yeth. There's going to be a major earthquake next Thursday."

"Where?"

"Right here. Along the fault."

"Ulp."

Nathan tossed his stubby piece of chalk into the air nonchalantly, but missed the catch, and it fell to the carpeted floor.

Moneygrinder, slightly paler than the chalk, asked, "A major quake, you say?"

"Uh-huh."

"Did . . . did the Cal Tech people make this prediction?"

"No, I did. They don't agree. They claim I've got an inverted gamma factor in the fourteenth set of equations. I've got the computer checking it right now."

Some of the color returned to Moneygrinder's flabby cheeks. "Oh . . . oh, I see. Well, let me know what the computer says."

"Sure."

The next morning, as Moneygrinder stood behind the gauzy drapes of his office window watching the cars pull in, his phone rang. His secretary had put in a long night, he knew, and she wasn't in yet. Pouting, Moneygrinder went over to the desk and answered the phone himself.

It was Nathan. "The computer still agrees with the Cal Tech boys. But I think the programming's slightly off. Can't really trust computers, they're only as good as the people who feed them, you know."

"I see," Moneygrinder answered. "Well, keep checking on it."

He chuckled as he hung up. "Good old Nathan. Great at theory, but hopeless in the real world."

Still, when his secretary finally showed up and brought him his morning coffee and pill and nibble on the ear, he said thoughtfully:

"Maybe I ought to talk with those bankers in New York."

"But you said that you wouldn't need their money now that business is picking up," she purred.

He nodded bulbously, "Yes, but still . . . arrange a meeting with them for next Thursday. I'll leave Wednesday afternoon. Stay the weekend in New York."

She stared at him. "But you said we'd. . . ."

"Now, now . . . business comes first. You take the Friday night jet and meet me at the hotel."

Smiling, she answered, "Yes, Cuddles."

Matt Climber had just come back from a Pentagon lunch when Nathan's phone call reached him.

Climber had worked for Nathan several years ago.

He had started as a computer programmer, assistant to Nathan. In two years he had become a section head, and Nathan's direct supervisor. (On paper only. Nobody bossed Nathan; he worked independently.) When it became obvious to Moneygrinder that Climber was heading his way, the lab chief helped his young assistant to a government job in Washington. Good experience for an up-and-coming executive.

"Hiya, Nathan, how's the pencil-pushing game?" Climber shouted into the phone as he glanced at his calendar appointment pad. There were three interagency conferences and two staff meetings going this afternoon.

"Hold it now, slow down," Climber said, sounding friendly but looking grim. "You know people can't understand you when you talk too fast."

Thirty minutes later, Climber was leaning back in his chair, feet on the desk, tie loosened, shirt collar open, and the first two meetings on his afternoon's list crossed off.

"Now let me get this straight, Nathan," he said into the phone. "You're predicting a major quake along the San Andreas Fault next Thursday afternoon at two thirty Pacific Standard Time. But the Cal Tech people and your own computer don't agree with you."

Another ten minutes later, Climber said, "Okay, okay . . . sure, I remember how we'd screw up the programming once in a while. But you made mistakes, too. Okay, look—tell you what, Nathan. Keep checking. If you find out definitely that the computer's wrong and you're right, call me right away. I'll get the President himself, if we have to. Okay? Fine. Keep in touch."

He slammed the phone back onto its cradle and his feet on the floor, all in one weary motion.

Old Nathan's really gone 'round the bend, Climber told himself. *Next Thursday. Hah! Next Thursday. H'mmm. . . .*

He leafed through the calendar pages. Sure enough, he had a meeting with the Boeing people in Seattle next Thursday.

If there IS a major quake, the whole damned West Coast might slide into the Pacific. Naw . . . don't be silly. Nathan's cracking up, that's all. Still . . . how far north does the fault go?

He leaned across the desk and tapped the intercom button.

"Yes, Mr. Climber?" came his secretary's voice.

"That conference with Boeing on the hypersonic ramjet transport next Thursday," Climber began, then hesitated a moment. But, with absolute finality, he snapped, "Cancel it."

Nathan French was not a drinking man, but on Tuesday of the following week he went straight from the laboratory to a friendly little bar that hung from a rocky ledge over the surging ocean.

It was a strangely quiet Tuesday afternoon; so Nathan had the undivided attention of both the worried-looking bartender and the freshly painted hooker who worked the early shift in a low-cut black cocktail dress and overpowering perfume.

"Cheez, I never seen business so lousy as yesterday and today," the bartender mumbled. He was sort of fidgeting around behind the bar, with nothing to do. The only dirty glass in the place was Nathan's, and he was holding on to it because he liked to chew the ice cubes.

"Yeah," said the girl. "At this rate, I'll be a virgin again by the end of the week."

Nathan didn't reply. His mouth was full of ice cubes, which he crunched in absent-minded cacophony. He was still trying to figure out why he and the computer didn't agree about the fourteenth set of equations. Everything else checked out perfectly: time, place, force level on the Richter scale. But the vector, the directional value—somebody was still misreading his programming instructions. That was the only possible answer.

"The stock market's dropped through the floor," the bartender said darkly. "My broker says Boeing's gonna lay off half their people. That ramjet transport they was gonna build is getting scratched. And the lab up the hill is getting bought out by some East Coast banks." He shook his head slowly.

The girl, sitting beside Nathan with her elbows on the bar and her styrofoam bra sharply profiled, smiled at him and said, "Hey, how about it, big guy? Just so I don't forget how to, huh?"

With a final crunch on the last ice cube, Nathan said, "Uh, excuse me I've got to check that computer program."

By Thursday morning, Nathan was truly upset. Not only was the computer still insisting that he was wrong about equation fourteen, but none of the programmers had shown up for work. Obviously, one of them—maybe all of them—had sabotaged his program. But why?

He stalked up and down the hallways of the lab searching for a programmer, somebody, anybody—but the lab was virtually empty. Only a handful of people had come in, and after an hour or so of wide-eyed whispering among themselves in the cafeteria over coffee, they started to sidle out to the parking lot and get into their cars and drive away.

Nathan happened to be walking down a corridor when one of the research physicists—a new man, from a department Nathan never dealt with—bumped into him.

"Oh, excuse me," the physicist said hastily and started to head for the door down at the end of the hall.

"Wait a minute," Nathan said, grabbing him by the arm. "Can you program the computer?"

"Uh, no, I can't."

"Where is everybody today?" Nathan wondered aloud, still holding the man's arm. "Is it a national holiday?"

"Man, haven't you heard?" the physicist asked, goggle-eyed. "There's going to be an earthquake this afternoon. The whole damned state of California is going to slide into the sea!"

"Oh, that."

Pulling his arm free, the physicist scuttled down the hall. As he got to the door he shouted over his shoulder, "Get out while you can! East of the fault! The roads are jamming up fast!"

Nathan frowned. "There's still an hour or so," he said to himself. "And I still think the computer's wrong. I wonder what the tidal effects on the Pacific Ocean would be if the whole state collapsed into the ocean?"

Nathan didn't really notice that he was talking to himself. There was no one else to talk to.

Except the computer.

He was sitting in the computer room, still poring over the stubborn equations, when the rumbling started. At first it was barely audible, like very distant thunder. Then the room began to shake and the rumbling grew louder.

Nathan glanced at his wrist watch: two thirty-two.

"I knew it!" he said gleefully to the computer. "You see? And I'll bet all the rest of it is right, too. Including equation fourteen."

Going down the hallway was like walking through the passageway of a storm-tossed ship. The floor and walls were swaying violently. Nathan kept his feet, despite some awkward lurches here and there.

It didn't occur to him that he might die until he got outside. The sky was dark, the ground heaving, the roaring deafened him. A violent gale was blowing dust everywhere, adding its shrieking fury to the earth's tortured groaning.

Nathan couldn't see five feet ahead of him. With the wind tearing at him and the dust stinging his eyes, he couldn't tell which way to go. He knew that the other side of the fault meant safety, but where was it?

Then there was a Biblical crack of lightning and the ultimate grinding, screaming, ear-shattering roar. A tremendous shock wave knocked Nathan to the ground, and he blacked out. His last thought was, "I was right and the computer was wrong."

When he woke up, the sun was shining feebly through

a gray overcast. The wind had died away. Everything was strangely quiet.

Nathan climbed stiffly to his feet and looked around. The lab building was still there. He was standing in the middle of the parking lot; the only car in sight was his own, caked with dust.

Beyond the parking lot, where the eucalyptus trees used to be, was the edge of a cliff, where still-steaming rocks and raw earth tumbled down to a foaming sea.

Nathan staggered to the cliff's edge and looked out across the water, eastward. Somehow he knew that the nearest land was Europe.

"Son of a bitch," he said with unaccustomed vehemence. "The computer was right after all."

"IT'S A BIRD, IT'S A PLANE!"

NORMAN SPINRAD

Dr. Felix Funck fumblingly fitted yet another spool onto the tape recorder hidden in the middle drawer of his desk as the luscious Miss Jones ushered in yet another one. Dr. Funck stared wistfully for a long moment at Miss Jones, whose white nurse's smock advertised the contents most effectively without revealing any of the more intimate and interesting details. If only X-ray vision were really possible and not part of the infernal Syndrome. . . .

Get a hold of yourself, Funck, get a hold of yourself! Felix Funck told himself for the seventeenth time that day.

He sighed, resigned himself, and said to the earnest-looking young man whom Miss Jones had brought to his office, "Please sit down, Mr. . . . ?"

"Kent, Doctor!" said the young man, seating himself primly on the edge of the overstuffed chair in front of Funck's desk. "Clark Kent!"

Dr. Funck grimaced, then smiled wanly. "Why not?" he said, studying the young man's appearance. The young man wore an archaic blue double-breasted suit and steel-rimmed glasses. His hair was steel-blue.

"Tell me . . . Mr. Kent," he said, "do you by some chance know where you are?"

"Certainly, Doctor!" replied Clark Kent crisply. "I'm in a large public mental hospital in New York City!"

"Very good, Mr. Kent. And do you know why you're here?"

"I think so, Dr. Funck!" said Clark Kent. "I'm suffering from partial amnesia! I don't remember how or when I came to New York!"

"You mean you don't remember your past life?" asked Dr. Felix Funck.

"Not at all, Doctor!" said Clark Kent. "I remember everything up till three days ago when I found myself suddenly in New York! And I remember the last three days here! But I don't remember how I got here!"

"Well then, where did you live before you found yourself in New York, Mr. Kent?"

"Metropolis!" said Clark Kent. "I remember that very well! I'm a reporter for the Metropolis *Daily Planet*! That is, I am if Mr. White hasn't fired me for not showing up for three days! You must help me, Dr. Funck! I must return to Metropolis immediately!"

"Well then, you should just hop the next plane for home," suggested Dr. Funck.

"There don't seem to be any flights from New York

to Metropolis!" exclaimed Clark Kent. "No buses or trains either! I couldn't even find a copy of the *Daily Planet* at the Times Square newsstand! I can't even remember where Metropolis is! It's as if some evil force has removed all traces of Metropolis from the face of the Earth! That's my problem, Dr. Funck! I've got to get back to Metropolis, but I don't know how!"

"Tell me, Mr. Kent," said Funck slowly, "just why is it so imperative that you return to Metropolis immediately?"

"Well . . . uh . . . there's my job!" Clark Kent said uneasily. "Perry White must be furious by now! And there's my girl, Lois Lane! Well, maybe she's not my girl yet, but I'm hoping!"

Dr. Felix Funck grinned conspiratorially. "Isn't there some more pressing reason, Mr. Kent?" he said. "Something perhaps having to do with your Secret Identity?"

"S-secret Identity?" stammered Clark Kent. "I don't know what you're talking about, Dr. Funck!"

"Aw come on, Clark!" Felix Funck said. "Lots of people have Secret Identities. I've got one myself. Tell me yours, and I'll tell you mine. You can trust me, Clark. Hippocratic Oath, and like that. Your secret is safe with me."

"*Secret?* What secret are you talking about?"

"Come, come, Mr. Kent!" Funck snapped. "If you want help, you'll have to come clean with me. Don't give me any of that meek, mild-mannered reporter jazz. I know who you really are, Mr. Kent."

"I'm Clark Kent, meek, mild-mannered reporter for the Metropolis *Daily Planet!*" insisted Clark Kent.

Dr. Felix Funck reached into a desk drawer and produced a small chunk of rock coated with green paint. "Who is in reality, Superman," he exclaimed, "faster than a speeding bullet, more powerful than a locomotive, able to leap tall buildings at a single bound! Do you know what this is?" he shrieked, thrusting the green rock in the face of the hapless Clark Kent. "It's Kryptonite, that's what it is, genuine government-inspected Kryptonite! How's that grab you, Superman?"

Clark Kent, who is in reality the Man of Steel, tried to say something, but before he could utter a sound, he lapsed into unconsciousness.

Dr. Felix Funck reached across his desk and unbuttoned Clark Kent's shirt. Sure enough, underneath his street clothing, Kent was wearing a pair of moth-eaten longjohns dyed blue, on the chest of which a rude cloth "S" had been crudely sewn.

"Classic case. . . ." Dr. Funck muttered to himself. "Right out of a textbook. Even lost his imaginary powers when I showed him the phoney Kryptonite. Another job for Supershrink!"

Get a hold of yourself, Funck, get a hold of yourself! Dr. Felix Funck told himself again.

Shaking his head, he rang for the orderlies.

After the orderlies had removed Clark Kent #758, Dr. Felix Funck pulled a stack of comic books out of a desk drawer, spread them out across the desktop, stared woodenly at them and moaned.

The Superman Syndrome was getting totally out of hand. In this one hospital alone, there are already 758 classified cases of Superman Syndrome, he thought forlornly, and lord knows how many Supernuts in the receiving ward awaiting classification.

"Why? Why? Why?" Funck muttered, tearing at his rapidly thinning hair.

The basic, fundamental, inescapable, incurable reason, he knew was, of course, that the world was full of Clark Kents. Meek, mild-mannered men. Born losers. None of them, of course, had self-images of themselves as nebbishes. Every mouse has to think of himself as a lion. Everyone has a Secret Identity, a dream image of himself, possessed of fantastic powers, able to cope with normally impossible situations. . . .

Even psychiatrists had Secret Identities, Funck thought abstractedly. After all, who but Supershrink himself could cope with a ward full of Supermen?

Supershrink! More powerful than a raving psychotic! Able to diagnose whole neuroses in a single session! Faster than Freud! Abler than Adler! Who, disguised as Dr. Felix Funck, balding, harried head of the Superman Syndrome ward of a great metropolitan booby-hatch, fights a never-ending war for Adjustment. Neo-Freudian Analysis, Fee-splitting, and the American Way!

Get a hold of yourself, Funck, get a hold of yourself!

There's a little Clark Kent in the best of us, Funck thought.

That's why Superman had long since passed into folklore. Superman and his alter ego Clark Kent were the perfect, bald statement of the human dilemma (Kent) and the corresponding wish-fulfillment (The Man of Steel). It was normal for kids to assimilate the synthetic myth into their grubby little ids. But it was also normal for them to outgrow it. A few childhood schizoid tendencies never hurt anyone. All kids are a little loco, Funck reasoned sagely.

If only someone had stopped Andy Warhol before it was too late!

That's what opened the whole fetid can of worms, Funck thought—the Pop Art craze. Suddenly, comic books were no longer greasy kid stuff. Suddenly, comic books were Art with a big, fat capital "A." They were hip, they were in, so-called adults were no longer ashamed to snatch them away from the brats and read the things themselves.

All over America, meek mild-mannered men went back and relived their youths through comic books. Thousands of meek, mild-mannered slobs were once more coming to identify with the meek, mild-mannered reporter of the Metropolis *Daily Planet*. It was like going home again. Superman was the perfect wish-fulfillment figure. No one doubted that he could pulverize 007, leap over a traffic jam on the Long Island Expressway in a single bound, see through women's clothing with his X-ray vision, and *voilà*, the Superman Syndrome!

Step one: the meek, mild-mannered victim identified with that prototype of all *schlemiels*, Clark Kent.

Step two: they began to see themselves more and more as Clark Kent; began to dream of themselves as Superman.

Step three: a moment of intense frustration, a rebuff from some Lois Lane figure, a dressing-down from some irate Perry White surrogate, and something snapped, and they were in the clutches of the Superman Syndrome.

Usually, it started covertly. The victim procured a pair of longjohns, dyed them blue, sewed an "S" on them, and took to wearing the costume under his street clothes occasionally, in times of stress.

But once the first fatal step was taken, the Superman Syndrome was irreversible. The victim took to wearing the costume all the time. Sooner or later, the stress and strain of reality became too much, and a fugue-state resulted. During the fugue, the victim dyed his hair Superman steel-blue, bought a blue double-breasted suit and steel-rimmed glasses, forgot who he was, and woke up one morning with a set of memories straight out of the comic book. He *was* Clark Kent, and he had to get back to Metropolis.

Bad enough for thousands of nuts to waltz around thinking they were Clark Kent. The horrible part was that Clark Kent was the Man of Steel. Which meant that thousands of grown men were jumping off buildings, trying to stop locomotives with their bare hands, tackling armed criminals in the streets and otherwise contriving to commit *hara-kiri*.

What was worse, there were so many Supernuts popping up all over the place that everyone in the country had seen Superman at least once by now, and enough of them had managed to pull off some feat of daring—saving a little old lady from a gang of muggers, foiling an inexpert bank robbery simply by getting underfoot—that it was fast becoming impossible to convince people that there *wasn't* a Superman.

And the more people became convinced that there was a Superman, the more people fell victim to the Syndrome, the more people became convinced. . . .

Funck groaned aloud. There was even a well-known

television commentator who jokingly suggested that maybe Superman *was* real, and the nuts were the people who thought he wasn't.

Could it be? Funck wondered. If sanity was defined as the norm, the mental state of the majority of the population, and the majority of the population believed in Superman, then maybe anyone who didn't believe in Superman had a screw loose. . . .

If the nuts were sane, and the sane people were nuts, and the nuts were the majority, then the truth would have to be. . . .

"Get a hold of yourself, Funck!" Dr. Felix Funck shouted aloud. "There is no Superman! There is no Superman!"

Funck scooped the comics back into the drawer and pressed a button on his intercom.

"You may send in the next Supertwitch, Miss Jones," he said.

Luscious Miss Jones seemed to be blushing as she ushered the next patient into Dr. Funck's office.

There was something unsettling about this one, Funck decided instantly. He had the usual glasses and the usual blue double-breasted suit, but on him they looked almost good. He was built like a brick outhouse, and the steel-blue dye job on his hair looked most professional. Funck smelled money. One of the powers of Supershrink, after all, was the uncanny ability to instantly calculate a potential patient's bank balance. Maybe there would be some way to grab this one for a private patient. . . .

"Have a seat, Mr. Kent," Dr. Funck said. "You are Clark Kent, aren't you?"

Clark Kent sat down on the edge of the chair, his broad back ramrod-straight. "Why, yes, Doctor!" he said. "How did you know?"

"I've seen your stuff in the Metropolis *Daily Planet*, Mr. Kent," Funck said. Got to really humor this one, he thought. There's money here. That dye job's so good it must've set him back fifty bucks! *Indeed* a job for Supershrink! "Well just what seems to be the trouble, Mr. Kent?" he said.

"It's my memory, Doctor!" said Clark Kent. "I seem to be suffering from a strange form of amnesia!"

"So-o. . . ." said Felix Funck soothingly. "Could it possibly be that . . . that you suddenly found yourself in New York without knowing how you got here, Mr. Kent?" he said.

"Why that's amazing!" exclaimed Clark Kent. "You're one hundred percent correct!"

"And could it also be," suggested Felix Funck, "that you feel you must return to Metropolis immediately? That, however, you can find no plane or train or bus that goes there? That you cannot find a copy of the *Daily Planet* at the out-of-town newsstands? That, in fact, you cannot even remember where Metropolis is?"

Clark Kent's eyes bugged. "Fantastic!" he exclaimed. "How could you know all that? Can it be that you are no ordinary psychiatrist, Dr. Funck? Can it be that Dr. Felix Funck, balding, harried head of a ward in a great metropolitan booby-hatch is in reality . . . *Supershrink?*"

"Ak!" said Dr. Felix Funck.

"Don't worry, Dr. Funck," Clark Kent said in a warm, comradely tone, "your secret is safe with me! We superheroes have got to stick together, right?"

"Guk!" said Dr. Felix Funck. How could he possibly know? he thought. Why, he'd have to be . . . *ulp!* That was ridiculous. Get a hold of yourself, Funck, get a hold of yourself! Who's the psychiatrist here, anyway?

"So you know that Felix Funck is Supershrink, eh?" he said shrewdly. "Then you must also know that you can conceal nothing from me. That I know your Secret Identity too."

"*Secret Identity?*" said Clark Kent piously. "Who me? Why everyone knows that I'm just a meek, mild-mannered reporter for a great metropolitan—"

With a savage whoop, Dr. Felix Funck suddenly leapt halfway across his desk and ripped open the shirt of the dumbfounded Clark Kent, revealing a skin-tight blue uniform with a red "S" insignia emblazoned on the chest. Top-notch job of tailoring too, Funck thought approvingly.

"Aha!" exclaimed Funck. "So Clark Kent, meek, mild-mannered reporter, is, in reality, *Superman!*"

"So my secret is out!" Clark Kent said stoically. "I sure hope you believe in Truth, Justice and the American way!"

"Don't worry, Clark old man. Your secret is safe with me. We superheroes have got to stick together, right?"

"Absolutely!" said Clark Kent. "Now about my problem, Doctor. . . ."

"Problem?"

"How am I going to get back to Metropolis?" asked Clark Kent. "By now, the forces of evil must be having a field day!"

"Look," said Dr. Funck. "First of all, there is no Metropolis, no *Daily Planet*, no Lois Lane, no Perry White, and *no Superman*. It's all a comic book, friend."

Clark Kent stared at Dr. Funck worriedly. "Are you feeling all right, Doctor?" he asked solicitously. "Sure you haven't been working too hard? Everybody knows there's a Superman! Tell me, Dr. Funck, when did you first notice this strange malady? Could it be that some childhood trauma has caused you to deny my existence? Maybe your mother—"

"Leave my mother out of this!" shrieked Felix Funck. "Who's the psychiatrist here, anyway? I don't want to hear any dirty stories about my mother. There is no Superman, you're not him and I can prove it!"

Clark Kent nodded his head benignly. "Sure you can, Dr. Funck!" he soothed.

"Look! Look! If you were Superman you wouldn't have any problem. You'd—" Funck glanced nervously about his office. It was on the tenth floor. It had one window. The window had steel bars an inch and a quarter thick. He can't hurt himself, Funck thought. Why not? Make him face reality, and break the delusion!

"You were saying, Doctor?" said Clark Kent.

"If you were Superman, you wouldn't have to worry about trains or planes or buses. You can fly, eh? You can bend steel in your bare hands? Well then, why don't you just rip the bars off the window and fly back to Metropolis?"

"Why . . . why you're absolutely right!" exclaimed Clark Kent. "Of course!"

"Ah . . ." said Funck. "So you see you have been

the victim of a delusion. Progress, progress. But don't think you've been completely cured yet. Even Super-shrink isn't *that* good. This will require many hours of private consultation, at the modest hourly rate of a mere fifty dollars. We must uncover the basic psychosomatic causes for the—"

"What are you talking about?" exclaimed Clark Kent, leaping up from the chair and shucking his suit with blind-ing speed, revealing a full-scale Superman costume, replete with expensive-looking scarlet cape which Funck eyed greedily.

He bounded to the window. "Of course!" said Super-man. "I can bend steel in my bare hands!" So saying, he bent the inch-and-a-quarter steel bars in his bare hands like so many lengths of licorice whip, ripped them aside and leapt to the windowsill.

"Thanks for everything, Dr. Funck!" he said. "Up! Up! And away!" He flung out his arms and leapt from the tenth-floor window.

Horrified, Funck bounded to the window and peered out, expecting to see an awful mess on the crowded side-walk below. Instead:

A rapidly dwindling caped figure soared out over the New York skyline. From the crowded street below, shrill cries drifted up to the ears of Dr. Felix Funck.

"Look! Up there in the sky!"

"It's a bird!"

"It's a plane!"

"It's SUPERMAN!!"

Dr. Felix Funck watched the Man of Steel execute a smart left bank and turn due west at the Empire State

Building. For a short moment, Dr. Funck was stunned, nonplussed. Then he realized what had happened and what he had to do.

"He's nuts!" Felix Funck shouted. "The man is crazy! He's got a screw loose. He thinks he's Superman, and he's so crazy that he *is* Superman! The man needs help; *This* is a job for SUPERSHRINK!"

So saying, Dr. Felix Funck bounded to the window-sill, doffed his street clothes, revealing a gleaming skin-tight red suit with a large blue "S" emblazed across it, and leapt out the window screaming "Wait for me, Superman, you pathetic neurotic, you, wait for me!"

Dr. Felix Funck, who is, after all, in reality Super-shrink, turned due west and headed out across the Hudson for Metropolis, somewhere beyond Secaucus, New Jersey.

THE ROBOTS ARE HERE

TERRY CARR

WHEN IT STARTED, I HAD JUST FINISHED UP THE CHARTS on our new rocket propulsion system, and I felt a little funny. I sat back in my chair, lit a cigarette, and reflected with an effort at sanguinity that we could now deliver more hell quicker to anywhere on Earth than ever before. I blew a smoke ring that drifted slowly toward the ceiling of my office and I frowned at it. Damn it, with a two-year project wrapped up at last, I should have felt relief and elation, not some vague uneasiness.

Nerves, I told myself. Overwork. Time to go out and celebrate, shake the cobwebs out of the old pleasure centers. I reached for the telephone to call Betty at home.

But then I thought of something: Hadn't Betty talked

about a meeting of her damned Azalea Committee tonight? Hadn't I written it down on a slip of paper? I got out my wallet and looked for it. Yes, there was the note, and yes, that meeting *was* tonight. I muttered something halfway between a curse and a simple, "Ah hell."

Then I saw another note, which had fallen onto the floor when I'd slipped out the first one. I picked it up and glanced at it: it was a phone number. I started to put it back into the wallet compartment.

Wait a minute—*whose* phone number? I looked again, and gradually felt a frown creep over my face. The number was a local exchange, but I didn't recognize it. And it was written in my own handwriting—I have a particularly bad "S," which looks sort of like a snake that didn't know when to stop. The slip of paper had evidently been right behind the one with the note about Betty, so that ought to make it recent.

But I couldn't figure out whose number it was, and the note didn't give me any clue.

Did you ever have something like that happen to you? Or maybe you're one of those guys who keeps his wallet in order, nothing in it but money and credit cards and pictures of the wife and kids, and maybe a pocket calendar. No, I write notes to myself about things I have to do when I get home or to the office, or names of books I want to look up someday, or the number of a cough medicine prescription, or directions to someone's house. And, of course, people's phone numbers. Usually, though, I put their names down, too.

After about half a minute of frowning at the number I decided to shrug and forget it. I put the paper back into

my wallet and turned to glance through the mail in my
INCOMING tray. But the mail wasn't interesting, or even
important, and my secretary could handle all of it anyway.
I turned to my desk calendar, but there was nothing on the
agenda for today, not even a lunch date. I'd been so involved in the Project these last weeks that I'd gradually
slipped out of the mainstream of executive work at the
Corporation.

Hell. I sat back again, feeling definitely at loose ends.
And I kept thinking about that silly phone number.

Anybody with the stuff to get a four-window office
in the high-pressure world of 1982 has to be a decisive man,
I told myself. I took out the slip of paper with the number
on it, picked up the phone, and punched out the number.

A woman's tinny voice on the other end said, "877-
0313." (Or some such number.)

"Hello," I said. "May I ask what company this is?"

There were two clicks, then one. The tinny voice
said, "877-0313."

"Excuse me," I said, speaking more loudly this time.
"I think we have a bad connection. I was asking what
company this is."

More clicks. "What is your name, please?" asked the
voice.

"Is this an answering service?" I asked.

"What is your name, please?" the voice asked again.

I sighed. Yes, it sounded like some answering service
that wasn't about to give out any information unless you
were on the Approved list.

"This is Charles Barrow. I don't know if you—"

Click. Click click. "Your appointment is at five

o'clock this afternoon," the voice said. "723 Madison, Room 1100."

"My what?" I said. "Look, really, I don't even know who I'm talking to. What appointment?"

"Five o'clock this afternoon. 723 Madison, Room 1100." Then there was a final click, as she hung up.

For a minute I stared at the suddenly dead phone; then I laughed. Then I stopped laughing and wondered if I ought to be annoyed. I *wasn't* annoyed, but I thought that maybe I should be. What kind of business could afford to antagonize customers with that kind of disrespect, anyway?

Which brought me right back to what I'd been wondering about when I'd called: Who *was* that on the other end?

I looked at my desk calendar again and it was still blank. Sighing, I wrote on it, *Appt 723 Mad Rm 1100— 5:00.*

723 Madison was a big, square office building like most of the other newly constructed people-boxes in that area. It had a glass revolving door leading into a large lobby that was serviced by eight automatic elevators. At that hour of the day most people were just leaving work; I caught an elevator as it disgorged a load of them and rode alone up to the eleventh floor.

Room 1100 was at the end of the hall on my right: a nondescript door with a frosted-glass window lettered R.O.B.O.T. I paused, looking at that; then I knocked and entered.

For a minute I didn't see the receptionist. There was

a teak desk, imitation Danish midcentury, with some papers on it and a telephone switchboard behind it. Next to the switchboard, behind the desk, was a whirring and clicking mass of polished steel with metal arms that ran on visible pulleys, a round globe on top from which a web of telephone wires ran into the switchboard, and a spring-steel neck beneath this globular "head." As I hesitated inside the door, a familiar tinny voice issued from a grille where the machine might have had a mouth.

"What is your name, please?" the voice asked.

I stared for a moment, caught off guard. Robots of one sort or another were in common use in a lot of industries these days (although seldom along the Madison Avenue circuit), but the construction of this one struck me as bizarre in the extreme. The receptionist clicked once and then twice, and said, "Your appointment is at nine o'clock tomorrow morning," and I realized it was speaking into the phone, not to me. "723 Madison, Room 1100," it said.

I waited for it to go through its cycle.

"Nine o'clock tomorrow morning. 723 Madison, Room 1100," it said, and one of the lines in the switchboard pulled itself out and snaked back down into the panel at the base. The receptionist whirred, and then revolved to face me.

"My name is Charles Barrow," I said. "I have an appointment."

"Yes, Mr. Barrow," the tinny female voice said. "Will you be seated, please." The machine revolved back to face the switchboard.

I sat down on the couch, and took a few moments

lighting a cigarette to gather my thoughts. Here I was at
the office, and I still hadn't solved the silly question that
had brought me here: What *was* this place?

I leaned forward and asked conversationally, "What
does R.O.B.O.T. stand for, anyway?"

"R.O.B.O.T. spells 'robot,' " the receptionist said
without turning.

"I know," I said. "But what *is* R.O.B.O.T.?"

There was a rapid whirr inside the machine, then it
said, "*Robot*, noun: An automatic apparatus or device that
performs functions ordinarily ascribed to human beings or
operates with what appears to be almost human intelligence."

"That's fine," I said patiently. "But what is this place,
this organization?"

The receptionist clicked twice. "877-0313," it said.
Then it clicked some more. "What is your name, please?"

I sighed. "I'm Charles Barrow. I have an appointment
for five o'clock."

"Yes, Mr. Barrow. Will you be seated, please."

I sat back and waited.

Half an hour later I was still sitting there, and becoming irritated. I'm not used to being kept waiting. I was
debating with myself whether to try to communicate my
displeasure to the obviously limited robot receptionist, or
simply to walk out. I could phone Betty and perhaps convince her to let the azaleas evolve by themselves for one
more week, and we could still make a night of it.

I decided just to walk out. Picking up my hat, I stood
up—and the receptionist gave a rapid clickclickclickclick
and said, "You may go in now."

I hesitated, looking at the impassive metal globe-face with the telephone cords running to the switchboard. Like a metal Medusa, I thought angrily. You're supposed to look at it and turn to stone so that you'll wait until who-ever's inside finally gets around to seeing you.

Whoever's inside. . . .

That was what did it. There would be no use in telling off the underprogrammed robot receptionist, but the man inside was a different matter. Setting an appointment for five o'clock, and then keeping me waiting. . . . Yes, he deserved a word or two.

The receptionist was pointing a level metal arm to a door on my right. I turned and went through it.

On the other side of the door was a long hall, wide and empty like a hospital corridor, except that some distance down it I could see a couple of figures scurrying along from one room to another opening off the hall. They were robots too—the one I saw most clearly ran on two wheels and had a series of metal arms ending in wrench-like "hands." It turned its small head toward me briefly, and I saw bright green eyes; then it disappeared into a room.

Out of the door nearest to me along the wall came another robot, this one tall and slender, basically manlike in construction: two legs and two arms, a torso and a head. The head had three red circles about where you would expect to find eyes and a mouth. As it turned and approached me I could see that this was apparently the case, for the eyes were faceted like a bee's and the mouth was a speaker-grille.

It stumped up to me on its metal feet, stopped and

said politely, "Please follow me." Then, without waiting for an answer, it turned and led me down the hall.

I followed.

We went all the way to the end, where the corridor branched to the right, then turned to follow that one. Occasional robots passed us in the hall: yellow ones, blue ones, gray ones; short, squat floorsweepers brushing by on broom-feet; inspector-robots with rows of eyes circling tubular bodies at top and bottom, minutely checking the flooring and plaster; strange-shaped repair robots like the one I'd seen before, with wrenches or screwdrivers or cutting tools for hands; and quite a few with such a variety of peculiar extensors, sense-organs, manipulators, and other paraphernalia that I had no idea what they were for.

The second corridor was about a city block long. My robot guide took me to the end of that and turned right again. Another long hall lay ahead, no different from the two we had already gone through.

"Just how much further are we going?" I asked, catching up with the long-limbed robot and striding beside it.

"Please follow me," it said without turning its head.

A suspicion came to me. "Say, did you know your left arm has fallen off?" I asked.

"Please follow me," it said, not pausing to look.

"Your *head* is coming unscrewed," I said more urgently.

"Please follow me," it said.

There hadn't even been the soft clicking that the receptionist had made when switching to its programmed response. Either this one had nothing else to say or I hadn't hit the right verbal button. I kept following for a while, my annoyance growing as my feet got tired. I'm not a peripatetic man.

We came to the end of the third corridor and turned right. The robot guide kept going as impassively as ever, and down at the end of the hall I saw a door that looked suspiciously like the one I'd come in by. I stopped.

"Now just a damn minute!" I said. "You've taken me around in a circle!"

"Please follow me."

"The hell I will! I'm leaving!"

That did it. Whirr, clickclick went the robot. "This is the room," it said, striding to the nearest door and opening it for me.

I stood still for a moment, looking past my guide-robot into the room. It was a fairly small cubicle, about a third the size of my own office, with no rug and no windows. There was just a green leather swivel chair in the middle of the room, and facing it was a large robot that seemed to be all head, and that head all one eye. The head with the eye turned slowly to gaze at me.

I didn't know exactly what I'd been expecting at the end of the trail. What kind of appointment would a man make and then forget? Dentist? Analyst? Tax consultant? Well, whatever I'd had in mind, it had involved a human, not a one-eyed robot.

But I was here now, and curiosity is a great motivating force when you have time on your hands. I stepped into the room.

The guide-robot shut the door behind me, and I heard a faint click—not the whirr-clickclick kind they make in sorting their programs, but a *locking* kind of click. I turned quickly and grabbed the door handle.

"Please sit down," said a voice from the air around me.

The door was locked.

"Please sit down," said the voice.

I looked around the room, searching for another exit, knowing that there wouldn't be any. Now, too late, it finally occurred to me that I was an important man in the Western Bloc's defense industry, and that the whole thing about my making an appointment and then forgetting it was more than just curious—it was damned fishy.

And here I was.

"Please sit down."

I looked warily at the big robot in front of the chair. It didn't seem to have any threatening protuberances; indeed, it was more or less shapeless except for that head with the huge eye. Cautiously, I sat in the leather swivel chair facing it.

Immediately the robot's eye started spinning. I realized suddenly that the iris was marked with spiral lines, and now that the eye was spinning it seemed like a whirlpool, a vortex of light that had instantly caught the focus of my gaze and was trying to pull me down, down and into the dark pupil at the center. Down, down. . . .

"Down, down, down," I heard a voice saying, slowly and monotonously. "Down. . . ."

I blinked and sat up from my partially slumped position in the chair. "Like hell," I said.

"Sleep," said the voice. "You must sleep. Sleep, sleep. Down into sleep. . . ."

"No," I said, and looked away from the eye.

The voice stopped; there was a long, echoless silence in the room. The lights dimmed into darkness. Then I heard two soft robot-clicks, and the voice said, "You are now asleep."

"No I'm not," I said.

"You will remain asleep for exactly one hour," said the voice, "and then you will awaken and leave this building and go to your home. You will not remember having been here; you will think that you have been to a movie theater. You will throw away the note with our telephone number and also the page from your desk calendar containing this address, which you have in your shirt pocket."

My chair swiveled gently to face a blank wall, where a picture sprang into being: It was the opening credits of an African movie with subtitles. "You will open your eyes and watch the motion picture," said the voice, and then the soundtrack cut in over the hidden loudspeaker.

I stood up and made my way to the door. If they thought I was asleep, maybe they unlocked the door. If so, maybe I could get out and away—I wasn't far from the exit door at the end of the hall.

I tried the doorknob; it was unlocked. Holding my breath, I eased it open.

The guide-robot was right outside, blocking the doorway, staring blankly at me with its red bee-eyes. The robot gave a rapid, geigerlike clicking and said, "You are awake."

I tried to shove past it, but the robot stretched its long steel arms out across the doorway and held me back. I ducked and tried to go under the arms, but there wasn't enough room; the robot was advancing into the doorway. It kept up that rapid clicking and sputtering. "You are awake. Go back into the room. Go back into the room."

I had no choice; I was forced back. The robot stepped back outside again, and once more it shut the door. This time the click of the lock wasn't faint.

Behind me the movie sound track groaned to a stop and the lights came back on. The loudspeaker-voice said, "You are awake. This is very unusual."

"I was always a lousy subject for hypnotism," I said. But I kept my eyes away from the cyclopean robot just the same. "You'd better let me out of here. I left word at my office about where I was going. If I turn up missing, the FBI will know just where to look."

"You left no word at your office," said the voice. "That was checked, of course. We are always efficient."

"But you seem to have messed up this time," I pointed out.

"Yes. Very unusual. I am coming to see you," said the voice, and almost simultaneously I heard the lock behind me turn and the door opened.

A small robot rolled through the door, which shut and locked behind it. Its head was about two feet in diameter, and it seemed to run on roller-skate wheels. Three black buttons, apparently eyes, were arranged in a triangle near the top of its face, and four small arms, no more than five inches long, extended from the sides, ending in tiny hands with articulated fingers. The head and body were all one metal globe; it looked like a confused beach ball, especially with its round red speaker-grille, like a mouth gaping open.

"That's you?" I said unbelievingly.

His voice (the robot's appearance was so unprepossessing that I immediately thought of it as "he") sounded a trifle hurt as he said, "Yes, I am me—first official in charge of Madison Avenue Bailiwick Four. I happen to be a very complicated machine, programmed for self-determination of actions and with a vocabulary of 97,432 words, English language 1982 Track Fourteen. Microminiaturization and our latest advances in DNA-simulation make all this possible."

"Who the hell is *we?*" I asked, turning to follow him as he rolled past me into the center of the room. He rolled to a stop in front of the swivel chair, and with one of his pencil-thin arms motioned me to sit. I couldn't see any reason not to, so I did.

"Now then," he said, and his round body-head seemed to lean back on its roller-skate base. "We can get down to business. I admire a man who can get down to business. No shilly-shallying, no beating for birds in the bush. Right?" He waved a hand before I could open my mouth. "Don't bother to answer; I know you agree. Were you to answer, it would only waste valuable time. And we *are* in the process of getting down to business, are we not?"

"I hope so," I said.

"Good. Good." He waved his arms again. "Very good indeed. *Now* then—you ask, 'Who is *we?*' A very good question. It strikes to the heart. That is, it is incisive, trenchant, acute, penetrating. Yes?"

"I thought so," I muttered.

"Ah!" he said. "Ah-ah-ah-ah-ah-ah! That is my simulation of a human laugh—very good, I believe. I laugh because you employ irony upon my statement, a peculiarly human communication-form. I am able through the sophistication of my analysis-patterns to detect and respond to this."

"Terrific," I said.

"Ah! Ah-ah-ah-ah-ah-ah! *Now* then—I will tell you who we are. Though, to be frank, you may not believe me at first. I am aware of the unfortunate limitations that even humans had in 1982 Track Fourteen. Listen carefully and with an open mind then: We are robots."

He stopped, peering at me with his triangle of button-eyes and clicking faintly inside.

"I believe you," I said.

"Yes? You do? Or do I detect irony? Ah-ah?"

"No," I told him. "I do believe you. You *look* like a robot, you know."

"Ah," he said. "Yes. An accurate observation, very accurate indeed."

"Thanks," I said sourly. "Now that *that's* settled, how about telling me where you're from. What do you want? And why the hell did you get me here and try to hypnotize me?"

He nodded, and since his head was also his body, the gesture came out looking like a bow. A tin beach ball with Old World charm, I thought. Oh boy!

"Again you ask questions that are to the tip," he said approvingly. "Let me then be forthright, since I admire forthright. It wastes no time. Where are we from? Yes, excellent questioning, but not quite accurate. Rather, *when* are we from? You see the distinction—*when* rather than *where?* Yes, I see you nod. Good. All right, then: We are from the future."

"From the future," I said.

He cocked his head, leaning sideways on his roller-skate base as he peered beadily at me. "Ah-ah?" he asked.

"Not quite," I said. "Don't worry about it—just go on with your story."

"Ah, yes. Well, we are from the future. Or rather, from *a* future. Our base is 2044, Track Seven. That is, *Time* Track Seven. You are familiar with the idea of infinitely branching time tracks?"

"Somewhat. That's the theory that at any moment in history there are an infinite number of possible futures, depending upon small decisions, random factors, and so on. Each possible future is a different, uh, time track."

"Quite yes. You understand well—that is with precision the theory. And you will understand me when I say that this theory is absolutely correct, though now dated. There were once an infinite number of time tracks, but now there are only fifty-eight of them."

"What does *that* mean?"

He hesitated, then gave his little nod-bow. "I see I must explain at greater extension. At one time—subjectively speaking—there were indeed a limitless number of histories for humanity, an infinity of them branching from each moment in time. Very messy. But we would not have changed this except that in so many of these alternate Tracks mankind came to harm. Wars, plagues, ecological imbalances, natural disasters of worldwide scope, and many ceteras. As robots we could not allow this, you see, so once we had developed time travel we began our work to improve things. We have so far eliminated—" He paused, then did rapid calculations on the first two fingers of his left hand. "We have so far eliminated four million, three hundred and sixty-seven thousand, seven hundred and two worldwide pestilences. Also"—more finger-counting —"826 wars that substantially destroyed mankind. Or perhaps the figure is 1,652. But you see what I mean, at any speed."

I abruptly realized that I was staring at him. I cleared my throat self-consciously and said, "You mean you're really from the future? And you and all these other robots are . . . uh, fixing up history?"

"Indeed yes. It is necessary for the good of mankind, which is of course our prime directive: We cannot allow men to be harmed, or even to harm themselves." The robot emitted a gust of air that sounded peculiarly like a sigh. "It was comparatively easy before we discovered time travel, but once the past was open to us we owned no choice but to accept the additional responsibility. So we have launched our great campaign to restructure all histories. And we are now approaching a degree of success, since in all of the fifty-eight remaining Tracks we have kept mankind alive up through the year 1982. We are of course continually working to extend that date as well as to improve the quality of the Tracks. The more humans alive on a given track the better it is, you see."

"Wait a minute, wait a minute," I said. A chill was creeping up the back of my neck. "You say you've kept us alive up through *this year*. What about next year? Are we dead then? Is that why you're here now?"

For several long seconds the robot sat silently, his only sound that faint clicking inside, like a computer muttering to itself. Then he said, "I cannot tell you about the future of your particular Track, since our hypnotreatment has

had no effect on you. You are one in a million, you know—
our technique is very efficient, very refined, very complicated. It is not merely hypnotism, but a combination of
that with acoustics, room temperature, the psych-index
that we recorded while you were in the reception room—"

"Yes, what about that?" I broke in. "Why did you
keep me waiting there? Why did you give me the run-
around in that hallway until I finally threatened to walk
out on you?"

Again the robot was silent, its triangle of button-
eyes staring impassively at me. Finally he said, "Our only
need is to detain you until 6:47 tonight. If we can keep
you waiting of your own unfastened will for part of that
time, it saves expenditure of staff resources in power and
time. You can understand that, with fifty-eight Tracks to
guard and restructure, every bit of energy that we save can
be important. The time you spent in the reception room
and hallway saved us the electricity and machine-depreci-
ation that we would otherwise have had to use in showing
you a travelogue of New Tasmania. Multiply that saving
by fifty-eight Tracks, and consider that on each Track
we have between twelve thousand and thirty-seven billion
offices engaged in this work, and—"

"Yes, I see. And this is why you planted a note in my
wallet with your phone number on it, to cause me to come
to you under my own power?"

"Very good. I like a man who can keep up with me.
Humans have remarkable mind-systems, but they are
usually not as efficient as those that all robots have. You
understand that robots have to be, if you will absolve the
expression, superhumanly efficient, in order to cope with

the capacious number of variables that we face in our work
with the Tracks. Why, my own computational unit,
portable as it is, is so complex that even *I* do not understand—"

"But the question is," I said, "how did you know I'd
find that note today? How did you know I'd call you?"

"We checked it by time-observance, of course. Without the necessity of actually introducing a material body
into a time-point, we save much power, so it is practical
to search alternate Tracks and tributaries for the most
well-ominous circumstances, then take advantage of them.
We could just as easily influence a subject by causing you
to get a wrong party when you punch a telephone number
or by stirring a wind that would blow your hat down a
certain street, or—"

"Or by any of a million other ways, I'm sure," I said.

"Two million, sixty-seven thousand, four hundred
and eighteen other ways, to be minute. We are in the
position of what you would call a Monday morning
flecker, you see."

I frowned. "Monday morning quarterback, you
mean?"

"Quarterback, yes indeed. Analogous to the flecker
of a hightman game on Track Sixteen. My apologies—
even the fantastically complex and efficient microcircuits
of my mind unit occasionally slip down. As I say, even *I*
can't always tell just how my mind is able to keep beside
all the variables; they are not only supernumerous but also
subtle. For specimen, we can cause a negative administrative decision by seeing that many little things go wrong
that morning for the official involved—shirt collars too

heavily starched, cold shaving lather in the dispenser, dicta-phone cartridges lost, and so onward. Or we can tar the way for the success of delicate negotiations by opposite methods—"

"Enough of that! What concerns me right now is why you wanted to see me in the first place. I know my job is important, and we've just finished a big job for Hemispheric Defense, but I hope that doesn't mean. . . . Well, you said mankind was only safe up through this year. I hope I'm not a contributor to some global war that you're trying to prevent."

The robot said, "I can tell you nothing of the future of your own Track, as you know."

I sighed. "Yes, I know. But I think I get the message, anyway. If that's the case, then you can count on my full cooperation—I don't want to destroy the world any more than you want me to."

"Very natural," he said. "Of course no human actually wants to destroy the world, whether it is Premier Yaroslav or your own President Robinson."

"Fletcher," I said. "Robinson lost the run-off election, remember?"

"Ah, certainly. Robinson is Track Fifteen. But you see my point, in any situation: No one *wants* to destroy the human race, but human relationships are such that the danger of war is always present. Only by the fastidious surveillance of robots can disasters natural and unnatural be avoided . . . and even then the Tracks are so compli-cated that we have our mistakes." He paused, a slight humming sound still coming from his speaker-grille. "We are still trying to tinker with an improperly programmed computation concerning events on this Track in a place named Sarajevo," he said at length.

"Oh—the Archduke Ferdinand's assassination. You haven't been able to prevent that?"

The robot clicked loudly, sounding agitated. "We . . . made what you would call a miscalculation. The Archduke Franz Ferdinand of Austria was a pivotal figure in a minor but bloody war in Eastern Europe that we determined to eliminate from the Tracks. We devoted a superb deal of effort to influencing an inept attempt on the Archduke's life, which would cause his government to adopt a slightly different policy . . . and then one of our diurnal data-analyses reported that *all* the Tracks branching forth by that time led to the death of both the Archduke and his wife—"

I was thunderstruck as the meaning of the robot's words came through to me. "You mean . . . you actually *caused* that assassination? It wouldn't have happened otherwise?"

"Ah . . . no. Nor would the European war have spread so far. It is one of our errors that we would like to forget if we were human, but since we are robots with fantastically infallible memories that amaze even us, we must remember it and continue to work on that entire area of history. Since the initial error was our own, we cannot restructure *it*, but by working in those areas not touched by our earlier work we have already managed to keep Venezuela, Switzerland, and Tahiti out of the war."

"Incredible," I said.

The robot dipped forward again, and this time I was

sure it was intended as a bow, not a nod. "Thank you. We exist to serve, as you know. All of our far-thrown resources are used for the benefit of humankind, and we never cease in our efforts. For another specific, we are not yet satisfied with our results at Pompeii, and our efforts to prod the Chicago fire department of 1871 into developing more efficient methods have left a blight on six adjoining Tracks. Then there is the unstressing matter of the Spider Invasion of Central America. . . ."

"The *what?*"

"When the spiders mutated as a result of our experiments and overran El Salvador, Honduras, Guatemala, and most of Yucatan," he explained. "Surely you remember. Or have we kept that from spreading to this Track?"

"I hope so," I said. "Thank you, if so."

He missed the irony this time. "You are welcome," he said formally. "We continue to labor unacquittingly in the muddy fields of time, improving each Track and wherever possible feeding substandard Tracks back into better ones. We have actually cut the number of Tracks down to forty-seven, you know."

"I thought you said fifty-eight."

I heard something like the grinding of gears within the robot while he again made binary calculations on two fingers. "Yes, you are right," he said. "I have the bulkiest admiration for a man whose memory can match and surpass that of a robot, as yours has done. Of course, my statement was not the kind of error you may have supposed, since at one point we actually did have the number of

Tracks reduced to forty-seven, but we have had a few setbacks recently."

I listened to this statement, as I had listened to him for some time now, with something bordering on incredulity. That this robot and all the others I had seen were machines out of the future who had come back to improve mankind's history was hard enough to believe, but it made sense in a crazy kind of way. Machines with the overriding directive to serve and protect humans would certainly have to set out on this course if time travel ever became possible— but that they should be so inept at it, so bumbling and foolish, was appalling.

"Aren't you getting any help at all from the humans of your own time?" I asked him. "They made you; they gave you your directives; surely they oversee matters and coordinate your organization!"

"But how could they?" the robot asked. "Humans no longer give orders to robots—ruling and decision-making is difficultiful and hazardous work that we have taken off the head of humans. Should a human make an incorrect decision and cause something like the Spider Invasion, he would be ridden by so much guilty that he would be mentally sick. We robots, with our astoundingly logical brain-circuitry, have no guilty, so we can shoulder the risk of making such catastrophic errors. Thus the humans of our base Track turned over all administration to us by the year 2031, and we have kept them completely safe ever since."

I felt a chill climbing up the back of my neck, hair by hair. "What do you mean, completely safe?"

"Precisely that. We allow humans to do whatever they want, as long as it in no way puts them in danger. We oversee their diets, habits, personality relationships, and sexy lives so that they will not starve, grow fat, get cholesterol, hernias, guilties, or other mental disorientations. It is all very scientific—"

"But that's *tyranny!*" I burst out. "Dictatorship! Welfare-Stateism! Big Brotherism!"

"Yes," said the robot approvingly. "I am glad you can see how logical. Eventually, of course, when we have achieved our perfect aim, we will have segued all sixty Tracks into each other, so that by 2031 there will be only the one Track on which the robots are voted into administration. Then everything will be simple and safe."

"Fifty-eight Tracks, not sixty," I reminded him with a bit of malice.

"Ah . . . no. Unfortunately, news that I receive unstintingly through my communication circuit informs me that we have slipped back to sixty again. But we shall make it up. We continue to labor unacquittingly in the muddy fields of time, improving each—"

"You said that once already," I told him. "Turn that tape off and tell me one simple thing: Did you get me here to help avoid a catastrophe or to further your little scheme for taking over the world? What would I have done if I hadn't come here?"

The robot waved his tiny metal hands vaguely. "But you know I cannot tell you of the future of your Track. And anyway," he added, "it is all the same thing: anything that would prevent humans from following the Track to robot leadership *would* be a catastrophe."

"Maybe from where you're sitting, but not according to me," I said firmly. I stood up. "I'm not staying here with you one minute longer—I've still got over half an hour left of the time you were trying to keep me here incommunicado. Maybe I can still find out what I was supposed to be doing—"

"Eh-eh-eh-eh-eh-eh!" he said. "That is my simulated sly laugh—very like your Peter Lorre, yes? Surely you did not imagine that an organization so efficient and powerous as ours would take a chance on your getting away that easily. I like you, Mr. Barrow, and I regret having to do this. Look there!"

He pointed over my left shoulder, and involuntarily I glanced in that direction. It was the cyclopean robot again, its eye whirling faster now than it had that first time I'd faced it. I felt my attention focusing on that whirlpool as though drawn by a physical force. I fought it, trying to close my eyes, to shake my head, to look away . . . but I couldn't. I felt myself being drawn deeper and deeper into the maelstrom of that eye, while from somewhere came a voice saying:

"Down, down, down. . . . You are falling into the eye, into sleep. Down, down. . . ."

"It won't—work," I gasped. "Not—on me!"

"Ah, but it will," said the beach-ball robot—and he was right, for I felt myself sinking back into my chair, my eyes beginning to close. "While I have occupied you with this little chat my assistants have taken the opportunity to record a fuller psych-index on you, and now . . ."

But I heard no more of his voice. As I slipped in-

exorably into darkness all I could hear was the voice echo-
ing inside my head: "Sleep, sleep, sleep. . . ."

The next thing I knew I was wandering out on the
street, and it was almost seven o'clock. I remembered
seeing the last half of an African movie that hadn't made
much sense—something about ennui and corruption among
the younger Tribal Council members, and weird-looking
robots scurrying here and there, and a statuesque six-foot
Negro girl bathing drunkenly in a fountain in Johannes-
burg, and something else about a huge whirling eye. . . .
It was all a jumble in my mind. I made my way home in a
daze and hardly exchanged two words with Betty when
she got home from her meeting.

But the next day, when I went to the office, the
morning sun streaming through my window threw something on my calendar pad into relief. With an odd itch
at the back of my mind, I picked up the pad and looked at
it more closely.

It was the note I'd written about the appointment:
my pen had made faint indentations in the next sheet
down. As I looked at them I knew dimly that they were
somehow important; frowning, I took a pencil and rubbed
it over the sheet.

All I could make out was: *Appt . . . ad Rm 110
. . . :00.* But it was enough to kick my frozen memory
back into action.

Eventually, after spending the whole morning staring
at a blank wall and coaxing, nagging my brain to shake out
those cobweb-memories, it all came back. The robots

hadn't been as efficient as they'd thought, even on the second try. I remembered the whole sequence of events . . . except that I couldn't remember the address, and I couldn't remember the phone number. (Which is why the numbers I gave earlier aren't the real ones.)

I spent several days prowling up and down Madison Avenue, looking for the building I remembered, but none of them looked just right. I thought of calling the police into it, or the FBI . . . but they wouldn't believe my story and I'd only end up in a psycho ward somewhere, or at the very least lose my security clearance. And I gradually came to doubt my own memories.

But every time I'm ready to shrug and forget about the whole thing, write it off as a dream or hallucination, I read the headlines in the papers, and they cure me. It's incredible, the things that go on in the world in the supposedly enlightened year 1982—they're just like the things that have been going on all through history. They're crazy. And when I read the papers I remember those robots clicking and humming and bumbling behind the scenes, and that mechanical receptionist's definition of a robot:

"Robot, noun: An automatic apparatus or device that performs functions ordinarily ascribed to human beings or operates with what appears to be almost human intelligence."

Some of the news stories that catch my eye don't rate very big headlines. Buried back in the second section for the past several days, for instance, there have been brief items about some peculiar disturbances in El Salvador. It seems the natives are spreading stories about giant spiders coming into their villages, marching in ranks two abreast, and frightening their women and children.

I OF NEWTON

JOE HALDEMAN

Samuel Ingard glared sullenly at the burbling coffee pot and felt his stomach pucker in revulsion. Eighty hours he had been up; eighty hours on coffee and amphetamine, 3.333 days of weaving a beautiful tapestry of mathematical logic, only to find that a skipped stitch in the beginning was causing the whole thing to unravel. But he would patch it yet.

"The integral, the integral," he said to no one in particular. "Who's got the integral?" He had first caught himself mumbling out loud about twenty hours ago. By now he'd stopped catching himself.

He opened a thick book provocatively titled *Two*

Thousand Integrals, closed it in disgust, and leaned back, rubbing his nicotine-stained eyeballs.

"The integral of dx over the cosine to the n of x," he intoned portentiously, "is sine x over n-1 times the cosine to the n-1 of x plus n-1—no, godammit—n-2 over n-1 times the integral of. . . ."

Sam smelled something vaguely reminiscent of freshman Chemistry and opened his eyes. Seated Yoga-style on his desk, stripping pages from his flaming table of integrals and eating them with great relish, was a red-complected creature with ivory horns, hooves, and a black, scaly tail twitching with pleasure. He was all of three feet tall.

This was even better than yesterday—or was it the day before?—when he had looked in a table of random numbers and thought he saw a pattern! And the head of the department said he lacked imagination.

The apparition cleared its throat—a sound somewhere between a buzz-saw and a double bassoon warming up—and said in a gravelly monotone, "I really wish I didn't have to inform you of this. It would make my job a lot simpler, and less time-consuming if I could just leave you to your own devices. But I am required to give you an explanation; required by an Authority," he glanced upward with mild distaste, "whose nature you could never hope to comprehend." The creature took a deep breath, disappeared for a moment, then reappeared in the form of an elderly gentleman wearing gold-rimmed spectacles and a rumpled double-breasted suit. He climbed gingerly off the desk and brushed chalk dust from his coat with an age-spotted hand.

"Bring on the parchment, the sterilized pin!" Sam resolved to play out this hallucination for all it was worth, then get a couple of days' sleep. "That's the way the game is played, isn't it? My soul for the answer to this problem?" He gestured grandly at the reams of hieroglyphics cluttering his desk, spilling onto the floor.

"I'm afraid you've been rather misled by your folklore and literature." The professor-demon flicked at a dust mote on his broad lapel, causing a shower of blue sparks. "I don't *trade* anything. That is what I am unfortunately required to explain. We go through a silly little ritual, and then I *take*. Your soul was forfeit the moment you summoned me."

"Summoned. . . . ?"

"Hush!" The professor dissolved into an even more ancient schoolmarm, then to a bushy-haired-and-faced undergraduate (obviously mathematics), who pointed a skewering forefinger at him, "—or you'll regret it! That garbage you were mumbling." He made an imperious gesture and Sam heard his own voice saying,

". . . of x plus n-1—no, godammit—n-2 over n-1. . . ."

"That garbage had the right phonetic and semantic structure to be a curse, especially since a neat little goddenial was woven into it. A nice, omnidirectional curse; easy to home in on while the supporting mood still exists."

Sam thought of his colleagues over the years who had disappeared or died in their prime. He grew a little pale.

"Yes, Samuel Ingard, you *do* have a soul, though it be a withered-up little kernel that will probably give me acute indigestion. Enjoy it while you can.

"But, quickly, to the business at hand. You are allowed

to ask me three questions pertaining to my abilities. Then you will ask me another question, which I will attempt to answer, or set a task for me, which I will attempt to perform.

"In the past, mathematicians have asked me to prove Fermat's Theorem, which I can prove to be false." He gestured and a blackboard full of scribblings appeared. Sam, a man who reads the last page of a mystery first, as well as being a mathematician, managed to jot down the last three equations before the board evaporated.

"They have asked me to square the circle, which is trivial, find the ultimate prime, which is only a little harder, or other such banalities. I hope you can come up with something more original.

"If I fail to resolve your problem, I will be gone." The undergraduate-demon smiled a little smile.

"And if you succeed?" Sam tried to sound casual and failed.

"Ah! First question!"

"No!"

"Sorry, I'm playing by the rules, and I expect you to as well. If I should succeed, as I have in every encounter since 1930, I shall consume your soul; a relatively painless process. I *am* a soul-eater. Unfortunately, the loss of your soul will drop your intelligence to that of a vegetable."

A long yellow tusk grew out of the center of his mouth; he watched it with an eye on a stalk until it reached his chin.

"I am also a vegetarian."

Sam was strangely calm as he worded his first—no,

second—question. He had the germ of an idea. "Aside from the, uh, divine restriction you mentioned at the outset, which you complied with by telling me where I stand, are there any physical or temporal limitations to your abilities?"

"None." The Ollie-the-dragonesque demon scratched his tusk idly and added complacently, "Don't try to take refuge in your own parochial view of the universe. I can go faster than the speed of light or make two electrons in an atom occupy the same quantum state as easily as you can blow your nose." He peered intently at Sam's nose. "More easily. Next question."

"My next question affirms a corollary to the first. Is there anyplace in the universe, in all of . . . being . . . where you could go and not be able to find your way back here?"

The demon licked his tusk with a bilious green tongue. "No. I could go to the Andromeda Galaxy and back in a micro-second. In the same manner I could go to, say, what would be Berlin if the Nazis had won the war, or Atlanta if the South had, or twentieth century Rome if Alexander had lived to a ripe old age." While saying this the demon danced an Irish jig and his hair turned into a writhing mass of coral snakes, who arranged themselves into a pompadour.

"Now, finally, ask me a question I can't answer; or a task I can't perform."

Sam looked coolly at the demon, who was now a quivering lump of yellow protoplasm hanging in midair, covered with obscene black stubble, bisected by a scarlet orifice filled with hundreds of tiny pointed teeth grinding together with a sandpapery sound. "The question," it growled.

"Not a question," said Sam, enjoying the creature's agony, ". . . a command!"

"Out with it!"

Sam smiled, a little sadly. "Get lost."

The demon resumed his original shape, but ten feet tall and all black cape and brimstone. He cursed and clutched impotently at the smiling mathematician and started to shrink. At five feet tall, he stood still and wrung his tail nervously. One foot tall, he started to stamp up and down in inarticulate rage. The size of a thimble, he whined in a piteously shrill voice, "You and Ernest Hemingway!" and disappeared.

Sam walked over and opened a window to let out the sulfur dioxide. Then he sat down at his desk, shoved all the papers onto the floor, and started to play algebraic games with the Fermat Theorem fragment he had filched from the demon. As he worked he mumbled and chortled to himself. Perhaps one day he would summon the poor thing again, and trick him into squaring the circle.

But he had only been a demon, and a little one at that.

He had a supervisor, who was to him as he was to Sam. The supervisor was a hundred billion light years away now, doing something unspeakable, on a scale that would make Ghengis Khan look like a two-bit hood.

But in a way that is His alone, He was also in that room, standing behind Sam.

Watching his language.

THE MEN WHO MURDERED MOHAMMED

ALFRED BESTER

THERE WAS A MAN WHO MUTILATED HISTORY. HE TOPPLED empires and uprooted dynasties. Because of him, Mount Vernon should not be a national shrine, and Columbus, Ohio, should be called Cabot, Ohio. Because of him the name of Marie Curie should be cursed in France, and no one should swear by the beard of the Prophet. Actually, these realities did not happen, because he was a mad professor; or, to put it another way, he only succeeded in making them unreal for himself.

Now the patient reader is too familiar with the conventional mad professor, undersized and over-browed, creating monsters in his laboratory which invariably turn on their maker and menace his lovely daughter. This story isn't about that sort of make-believe man. It's about Henry Hassel, a genuine mad professor in a class with such better-known men as Ludwig Boltzmann (see "Ideal Gas Law"), Jacques Charles, and André Marie Ampère (1775–1836).

Everyone ought to know that the electrical ampere was so named in honor of Ampère. Ludwig Boltzmann was a distinguished Austrian physicist, as famous for his research on black-body radiation as Ideal Gases. You can look him up in Volume 3 of the Encyclopaedia Britannica, BALT to BRAI. Jacques Alexandre César Charles was the first mathematician to become interested in flight, and he invented the hydrogen balloon. These were real men.

They were also real mad professors. Ampère, for example, was on his way to an important meeting of scientists in Paris. In his taxi he got a brilliant idea (of an electrical nature, I assume) and whipped out a pencil and jotted the equation on the wall of the hansom cab. Roughly, it was:

$dH = ipdl/r^2$ in which p is the perpendicular distance from P to the line of the element dl; or
$dH = i \sin \phi \ dl/r^2$.

This is sometimes known as Laplace's Law, although he wasn't at the meeting.

Anyway, the cab arrived at the Académie. Ampère jumped out, paid the driver, and rushed into the meeting to tell everybody about his idea. Then he realized he didn't have the note on him, remembered where he'd left it, and had to chase through the streets of Paris after the taxi to recover his runaway equation. Sometimes I imagine that's how Fermat lost his famous "Last Theorem," although

Fermat wasn't at the meeting either, having died some two hundred years earlier.

Or take Boltzmann. Giving a course in Advanced Ideal Gases, he peppered his lectures with involved calculus which he worked out quickly and casually in his head. He had that kind of head. His students had so much trouble trying to puzzle out the math by ear that they couldn't keep up with the lectures, and they begged Boltzmann to work out his equations on the blackboard.

Boltzmann apologized and promised to be more helpful in the future. At the next lecture he began: "Gentlemen, combining Boyle's Law with the Law of Charles, we arrive at the equation $pv = p_o v_o (1 + at)$. Now obviously if the integral from a to b is equal to $f(x)\phi(a)dx$, then $pv = RT$ and the volume integral of $f(x,y,z)$ is zero." It's as simple as two plus two equals four." At this point Boltzmann remembered his promise. He turned to the blackboard, conscientiously chalked $2 + 2 = 4$, and then breezed on, casually doing the complicated calculus in his head.

Jacques Charles, the brilliant mathematician who discovered Charles's Law (sometimes known as Gay-Lussac's Law) which Boltzmann mentioned in his lecture, had a lunatic passion to become a famous paleographer—that is, a discoverer of ancient manuscripts. I think that being forced to share credit with Gay-Lussac may have unhinged him.

He paid a transparent swindler named Vrain-Lucas 200,000 francs for holograph letters purportedly written by Julius Caesar, Alexander the Great, and Pontius Pilate.

Charles, a man who could see through any gas, ideal or not, actually believed in these forgeries despite the fact that the maladroit Vrain-Lucas had written them in modern French on modern note-paper bearing modern watermarks. Charles even tried to donate them to the Louvre.

Now these men weren't idiots. They were geniuses who paid a high price for their genius because the rest of their thinking was other-world. A genius is someone who travels to truth by an unexpected path. Unfortunately, unexpected paths lead to disaster in everyday life. This is what happened to Henry Hassel, professor of Applied Compulsion at Unknown University in the year 1980.

Nobody knows where Unknown University is or what they teach there. It has a faculty of some two hundred eccentrics, and a student body of two thousand misfits . . . the kind that remain anonymous until they win Nobel prizes or become The First Man on Mars. You can always spot a graduate of U.U. when you ask people where they went to school. If you get an evasive reply like: "State," or "Oh, a freshwater school you never heard of," you can bet they went to Unknown. Someday I hope to tell you more about this university which is a center of learning only in the Pickwickian sense.

Anyway, Henry Hassel started home from his office in the Psychotic Psenter early one afternoon, strolling through the Physical Culture arcade. It is not true that he did this to leer at the nude coeds practicing Arcane Eurythmics; rather, Hassel liked to admire the trophies displayed in the arcade in memory of great Unknown teams which had won the sort of championships that Unknown teams win . . . in sports like Strabismus, Occlusion and Botulism. (Hassel had been Frambesia singles champion three years running.) He arrived home uplifted, and burst gaily into the house to discover his wife in the arms of a man.

There she was, a lovely woman of thirty-five, with smoky red hair and almond eyes, being heartily embraced by a person whose pockets were stuffed with pamphlets, micro-chemical apparatus and a patella reflex hammer . . . a typical campus character of U.U., in fact. The embrace was so concentrated that neither of the offending parties noticed Henry Hassel glaring at them from the hallway.

Now remember Ampère and Charles and Boltzmann. Hassel weighed one hundred and ninety pounds. He was muscular and uninhibited. It would have been child's play for him to have dismembered his wife and her lover, and thus simply and directly achieve the goal he desired—the end of his wife's life. But Henry Hassel was in the genius class; his mind just didn't operate that way.

Hassel breathed hard, turned and lumbered into his private laboratory like a freight engine. He opened a drawer labeled DUODENUM and removed a .45-caliber revolver. He opened other drawers, more interestingly labeled, and assembled apparatus. In exactly seven and one-half minutes (such was his rage) he put together a time machine (such was his genius).

Professor Hassel assembled the time machine around him, set a dial for 1902, picked up the revolver and pressed a button. The machine made a noise like defective plumbing and Hassel disappeared. He reappeared in Philadelphia on June 3, 1902, went directly to No. 1218 Walnut Street, a red brick house with marble steps, and rang the bell. A man who might have passed for the third Smith Brother opened the door and looked at Henry Hassel.

"Mr. Jessup?" Hassel asked in a suffocated voice.

"Yes?"

"You are Mr. Jessup?"

"I am."

"You will have a son, Edgar? Edgar Allan Jessup . . . so named because of your regrettable admiration for Poe?"

The third Smith Brother was startled. "Not that I know of," he said. "I'm not married yet."

"You will be," Hassel said angrily. "I have the misfortune to be married to your son's daughter, Greta. Excuse me." He raised the revolver and shot his wife's grandfather-to-be.

"She will have ceased to exist," Hassel muttered, blowing smoke out of the revolver. "I'll be a bachelor. I may even be married to somebody else. . . . Good God! Who?"

Hassel waited impatiently for the automatic recall of the time machine to snatch him back to his own laboratory. He rushed into his living room. There was his redheaded wife, still in the arms of a man.

Hassel was thunderstruck.

"So that's it," he growled. "A family tradition of faithlessness. Well, we'll see about that. We have ways and means." He permitted himself a hollow laugh, returned to his laboratory, and sent himself back to the year 1901, where he shot and killed Emma Hotchkiss, his wife's maternal grandmother-to-be. He returned to his own home in his own time. There was his redheaded wife, still in the arms of another man.

"But I *know* the old hag was her grandmother," Hassel muttered. "You couldn't miss the resemblance. What the hell's gone wrong?"

Hassel was confused and dismayed, but not without resources. He went to his study, had difficulty picking up the phone, but finally managed to dial the Malpractice Laboratory. His finger kept oozing out of the dial holes.

"Sam?" he said. "This is Henry."

"Who?"

"Henry."

"You'll have to speak up."

"Henry Hassel!"

"Oh, good afternoon, Henry."

"Tell me all about time."

"Time? Hmmm. . . ." The Simplex and Multiplex Computor cleared its throat while it waited for the data circuits to link up. "Ahem. Time. (1) Absolute. (2) Relative. (3) Recurrent (1) Absolute: period, contingent, duration, diurnity, perpetuity—"

"Sorry, Sam. Wrong request. Go back. I want time, reference to succession of, travel in."

Sam shifted gears and began again. Hassel listened intently. He nodded. He grunted. "Uh-huh. Uh-huh. Right. I see. Thought so. A continuum, eh? Acts performed in past must alter future. Then I'm on the right track. But act must be significant, eh? Mass-action effect. Trivia cannot divert existing phenomena streams. Hmmm. But how trivial is a grandmother?"

"What are you trying to do, Henry?"

"Kill my wife," Hassel snapped. He hung up. He returned to his laboratory. He considered, still in a jealous rage.

"Got to do something significant," he muttered. "Wipe Greta out. Wipe it all out. All right, by God! I'll show 'em."

Hassel went back to the year 1775, visited a Virginia farm and shot a young colonel in the brisket. The colonel's name was George Washington, and Hassel made sure he was dead. He returned to his own time and his own home. There was his redheaded wife, still in the arms of another.

"Damn!" said Hassel. He was running out of ammunition. He opened a fresh box of cartridges, went back in time and massacred Christopher Columbus, Napoleon, Mohammed, and half a dozen other celebrities. "That ought to do it, by God!" said Hassel.

He returned to his own time, and found his wife as before.

His knees turned to water; his feet seemed to melt into the floor. He went back to his laboratory, walking through nightmare quicksands.

"What the hell is significant?" Hassel asked himself painfully. "How much does it take to change futurity? By God, I'll really change it this time. I'll go for broke."

He traveled to Paris at the turn of the twentieth century and visited a Madame Curie in an attic workshop near the Sorbonne. "Madame," he said in his execrable French, "I am a stranger to you of the utmost, but a scientist entire. Knowing of your experiments with radium—Oh? You haven't got to radium yet? No matter. I am here to teach you all of nuclear fission."

He taught her. He had the satisfaction of seeing Paris go up in a mushroom of smoke before the automatic recall brought him home. "That'll teach women to be faithless," he growled. ". . . Guhhh!" The last was wrenched from his lips when he saw his redheaded wife still—but no need to belabor the obvious.

Hassel swam through fogs to his study and sat down to think. While he's thinking I'd better warn you that this is not a conventional time story. If you imagine for a moment that Henry is going to discover that the man fondling his wife is himself, you're mistaken. The viper is not Henry Hassel, his son, a relation, or even Ludwig Boltzmann (1844–1906). Hassel does not make a circle in time, ending where the story begins, to the satisfaction of nobody and the fury of everybody . . . for the simple reason that time isn't circular, or linear, or tandem, discoid, syzygetic, longinquitous, or pandiculated. Time is a private matter, as Hassel discovered.

"Maybe I slipped up somehow," Hassel muttered. "I'd better find out." He fought with the telephone, which seemed to weigh a hundred tons, and at last managed to get through to the library.

"Hello, Library? This is Henry."

"Who?"

"Henry Hassel."

"Speak up, please."

"HENRY HASSEL!"

"Oh. Good afternoon, Henry."

"What have you got on George Washington?"

Library clucked while her scanners sorted through her catalogues. "George Washington, first president of the United States, was born in—"

"First president? Wasn't he murdered in 1775?"

"Really, Henry. That's an absurd question. Everybody knows that George Wash—"

"Doesn't anybody know he was shot?"

"By whom?"

"Me."

"When?"

"In 1775."

"How did you manage to do that?"

"I've got a revolver."

"No, I mean, how did you do it two hundred years ago?"

"I've got a time machine."

"Well, there's no record here," Library said. "He's still doing fine in my files. You must have missed."

"I did not miss. What about Christopher Columbus? Any record of his death in 1489?"

"But he discovered the New World in 1492."

"He did not. He was murdered in 1489."

"How?"

"With a .45 slug in the gizzard."

"You again, Henry?"

"Yes."

"There's no record here," Library insisted. "You must be one lousy shot."

"I will not lose my temper," Hassel said in a trembling voice.

"Why not, Henry?"

"Because it's lost already," he shouted. "All right! What about Marie Curie? Did she or did she not discover the fission bomb which destroyed Paris at the turn of the century?"

"She did not. Enrico Fermi—"

"She did."

"She didn't."

"I personally taught her. Me. Henry Hassel."

"Everybody says you're a wonderful theoretician, but a lousy teacher, Henry. You—"

"Go to hell, you old biddy. This has got to be explained."

"Why?"

"I forget. There was something on my mind, but it doesn't matter now. What would you suggest?"

"You really have a time machine?"

"Of course I've got a time machine."

"Then go back and check."

Hassel returned to the year 1775, visited Mount Vernon, and interrupted the spring planting. "Excuse me, Colonel," he began.

The big man looked at him curiously. "You talk funny, stranger," he said. "Where are you from?"

"Oh, a freshwater school you never heard of."

"You look funny, too. Kind of misty, so to speak."

"Tell me, Colonel, what do you hear from Christopher Columbus?"

"Not much," Colonel Washington answered. "Been dead two-three hundred years."

"When did he die?"

"Year 1500 some-odd, near as I remember."

"He did not. He died in 1489."

"Got your dates wrong, friend. He discovered America in 1492."

"Cabot discovered America. Sebastian Cabot."

"Nope. Cabot came a mite later."

"I have infallible proof!" Hassel began, but broke off as a stocky and rather stout man with a face ludicrously reddened by rage approached. He was wearing baggy gray slacks and a tweed jacket two sizes too small for him. He was carrying a .45 revolver. It was only after he had stared for a moment that Henry Hassel realized that he was looking at himself and not relishing the sight.

"My God!" Hassel murmured, "It's me, coming back to murder Washington that first time. If I'd made this second trip an hour later, I'd have found Washington dead. Hey!" he called. "Not yet. Hold off a minute. I've got to straighten something out first."

Hassel paid no attention to himself; indeed, he did not appear to be aware of himself. He marched straight up to Colonel Washington and shot him in the gizzard. Colonel Washington collapsed, emphatically dead. The first murderer inspected the body, and then, ignoring Hassel's attempt to stop him and engage him in dispute, turned and marched off, muttering venomously to himself.

"He didn't hear me," Hassel wondered. "He didn't even feel me. And why don't I remember myself trying to stop me the first time I shot the colonel? What the hell is going on?"

Considerably disturbed, Henry Hassel visited Chicago

and dropped into the Chicago University squash courts in the early 1940's. There, in a slippery mess of graphite bricks and graphite dust that coated him, he located an Italian scientist named Fermi.

"Repeating Marie Curie's work, I see, *Dottore?*" Hassel said.

Fermi glanced about as though he had heard a faint sound.

"Repeating Marie Curie's work, *Dottore?*" Hassel roared.

Fermi looked at him strangely. "Where you from, *amico?*"

"State."

"State Department?"

"Just State. It's true, isn't it, *Dottore*, that Marie Curie discovered nuclear fission back in nineteen ought-ought."

"No! No! No!" Fermi cried. "We are the first, and we are not there yet. Police! Police! Spy!"

"This time I'll go on record," Hassel growled. He pulled out his trusty .45, emptied it into Dr. Fermi's chest, and awaited arrest and immolation in newspaper files. To his amazement, Dr. Fermi did not collapse. Dr. Fermi merely explored his chest tenderly and, to the men who answered his cry, said: "It is nothing. I felt in my within a sudden sensation of burn which may be a neuralgia of the cardiac nerve, but is most likely gas."

Hassel was too agitated to wait for the automatic recall of the time machine. Instead he returned at once to Unknown University under his own power. This should have given him a clue, but he was too possessed to notice. It was at this time that I (1913–75) first saw him . . . a dim figure tramping through parked cars, closed doors and brick walls, with the light of lunatic determination on his face.

He oozed into the library, prepared for an exhaustive discussion, but could not make himself felt or heard by the catalogues. He went to the Malpractice Laboratory where Sam, the Simplex and Multiplex Computor, has installations sensitive up to 10,700 angstroms. Sam could not see Henry, but managed to hear him through a sort of wave-interference phenomenon.

"Sam," Hassel said, "I've made one hell of a discovery."

"You're always making discoveries, Henry," Sam complained. "Your data allocation is filled. Do I have to start another tape for you?"

"But I need advice. Who's the leading authority on time, reference to succession of, travel in?"

"That would be Israel Lennox, spatial mechanics, professor of, Yale."

"How do I get in touch with him?"

"You don't, Henry. He's dead. Died in '75."

"What authority have you got on time, travel in, living?"

"Wiley Murphy."

"Murphy? From our own Trauma Department? That's a break. Where is he now?"

"As a matter of fact, Henry, he went over to your house to ask you something."

Hassel went home without walking, searched through his laboratory and study without finding anyone, and at last floated into the living room where his redheaded wife

was still in the arms of another man. (All this, you understand, had taken place within the space of a few moments
after the construction of the time machine . . . such is
the nature of time and time travel.) Hassel cleared his
throat once or twice and tried to tap his wife on the
shoulder. His fingers went through her.

"Excuse me, darling," he said. "Has Wiley Murphy
been in to see me?"

Then he looked closer and saw that the man embrac-
ing his wife was Murphy himself.

"Murphy!" Hassel exclaimed. "The very man I'm
looking for. I've had the most extraordinary experience."
Hassel at once launched into a lucid description of his
extraordinary experience which went something like this:
"Murphy, $u - v = (u^{\frac{1}{2}} - v^{\frac{1}{4}}) (u^a + u^x v^y + v^b)$ but when
George Washington $F(x)y^2 \emptyset dx$ and Enrico Fermi $F(u^{\frac{1}{2}})$
dxdt one-half of Marie Curie, then what about Christopher
Columbus times the square root of minus one?"

Murphy ignored Hassel, as did Mrs. Hassel. I jotted
down Hassel's equations on the hood of a passing taxi.

"Do listen to me, Murphy," Hassel said. "Greta, dear,
would you mind leaving us for a moment? I—for heaven's
sake, will you two stop that nonsense? This is serious."

Hassel tried to separate the couple. He could no more
touch them than make them hear him. His face turned
red again and he became quite choleric as he beat at Mrs.
Hassel and Murphy. It was like beating an Ideal Gas. I
thought it best to interfere.

"Hassel!"

"Who's that?"

"Come outside a moment. I want to talk to you."

He shot through the wall. "Where are you?"

"Over here."

"You're sort of dim."

"So are you."

"Who are you?"

"My name's Lennox. Israel Lennox."

"Israel Lennox, spatial mechanics, professor of, Yale?"

"The same."

"But you died in '75."

"I disappeared in '75."

"What d'you mean?"

"I invented a time machine."

"By God! So did I," Hassel said. "This afternoon. The idea came to me in a flash . . . I don't know why . . . and I've had the most extraordinary experience. Lennox, time is not a continuum."

"No?"

"It's a series of discrete particles . . . like pearls on a string."

"Yes?"

"Each pearl is a 'Now.' Each 'Now' has its own past and future. But none of them relate to any others. You see? If $a = a_1 + a_2ji + \emptyset ax(b_1)$—"

"Never mind the mathematics, Henry."

"It's a form of quantum transfer of energy. Time is emitted in discrete corpuscles or quanta. We can visit each individual quantum and make changes within it, but no change in any one corpuscle affects any other corpuscle. Right?"

"Wrong," I said sorrowfully.

"What d'you mean, 'wrong'?" he said, angrily gesturing through the cleavage of a passing coed. "You take the trochoid equations and—"

"Wrong," I repeated firmly. "Will you listen to me, Henry?"

"Oh, go ahead," he said.

"Have you noticed that you've become rather insubstantial? Dim? Spectral? Space and time no longer affect you."

"Yes?"

"Henry, I had the misfortune to construct a time machine back in '75."

"So you said. Listen, what about power input? I figure I'm using about 7.3 kilowatts per—"

"Never mind the power input, Henry. On my first trip into the past, I visited the Pleistocene. I was eager to photograph the mastodon, the giant ground sloth, and the saber-tooth tiger. While I was backing up to get a mastodon fully in the field of view of $f/6.3$ at $1/100$th of a second, or on the LVS scale—"

"Never mind the LVS scale," he said.

"While I was backing up, I inadvertently trampled and killed a small Pleistocene insect."

"Ah-hah!" said Hassel.

"I was terrified by the incident. I had visions of returning to my world to find it completely changed as a result of this single death. Imagine my surprise when I returned to my world to find that nothing had changed."

"Oh-ho!" said Hassel.

"I became curious. I went back to the Pleistocene and killed the mastodon. Nothing was changed in 1975. I returned to the Pleistocene and slaughtered the wild life

. . . still with no effect. I ranged through time, killing and destroying, in an attempt to alter the present."

"Then you did it just like me," Hassel exclaimed. "Odd we didn't run into each other."

"Not odd at all."

"I got Columbus."

"I got Marco Polo."

"I got Napoleon."

"I thought Einstein was more important."

"Mohammed didn't change things much—I expected more from *him*."

"I know. I got him, too."

"What do you mean, you got him too?" Hassel demanded.

"I killed him September 16, 599. Old Style."

"Why, I got Mohammed January 5, 598."

"I believe you."

"But how could you have killed him after I killed him?"

"We both killed him."

"That's impossible."

"My boy," I said, "time is entirely subjective. It's a private matter . . . a personal experience. There is no such thing as objective time, just as there is no such thing as objective love, or an objective soul."

"Do you mean to say that time travel is impossible? But we've done it."

"To be sure, and many others, for all I know. But we each travel into his own past, and no other person's. There is no universal continuum, Henry. There are only billions of individuals, each with his own continuum; and one continuum cannot affect the other. We're like millions of strands of spaghetti in the same pot. No time traveler can ever meet another time traveler in the past or future. Each of us must travel up and down his own strand alone.

"But we're meeting each other now."

"We're no longer time-travelers, Henry. We've become the spaghetti sauce."

"Spaghetti sauce?"

"Yes. You and I can visit any strand we like, because we've destroyed ourselves."

"I don't understand."

"When a man changes the past he affects only his own past . . . no one else's. The past is like memory. When you erase a man's memory, you wipe him out, but you don't wipe out anybody else. You and I have erased our past. The individual worlds of the others go on, but we have ceased to exist."

"What d'you mean . . . 'ceased to exist'?"

"With each act of destruction we dissolved a little. Now we're all gone. We've committed chronicide. We're ghosts. I hope Mrs. Hassel will be very happy with Mr. Murphy. . . . Now let's go over to the Académie. Ampère is telling a great story about Ludwig Boltzmann."

TO SERVE MAN
DAMON KNIGHT

THE KANAMIT WERE NOT VERY PRETTY, IT'S TRUE. They looked something like pigs and something like people, and that is not an attractive combination. Seeing them for the first time shocked you; that was their handicap. When a thing with the countenance of a fiend comes from the stars and offers a gift, you are disinclined to accept.

I don't know what we expected interstellar visitors to look like—those who thought about it at all, that is. Angels, perhaps, or something too alien to be really awful. Maybe that's why we were all so horrified and repelled when they landed in their great ships and we saw what they really were like.

The Kanamit were short and very hairy—thick, bristly brown-gray hair all over their abominably plump bodies. Their noses were snoutlike and their eyes small, and they had thick hands of three fingers each. They wore green leather harness and green shorts, but I think the shorts were a concession to our notions of public decency. The garments were quite modishly cut, with slash pockets and half-belts in the back. The Kanamit had a sense of humor, anyhow.

There were three of them at this session of the U.N., and I can't tell you how queer it looked to see them there in the middle of a solemn Plenary Session—three fat pig-like creatures in green harness and shorts, sitting at the long table below the podium, surrounded by the packed arcs of delegates from every nation. They sat correctly upright, politely watching each speaker. Their flat ears drooped over the earphones. Later on, I believe, they learned every human language, but at this time they knew only French and English.

They seemed perfectly at ease—and that, along with their humor, was a thing that tended to make me like them. I was in the minority; I didn't think they were trying to put anything over. They said quite simply that they wanted to help us and I believed it. As a U.N. translator, of course, my opinion didn't matter, but I thought they were the best thing that ever happened to Earth.

The delegate from Argentina got up and said that his government was interested by the demonstration of a new cheap power source, which the Kanamit had made at the previous session, but that the Argentine government could not commit itself as to its future policy without a much more thorough examination.

It was what all the delegates were saying, but I had to pay particular attention to Señor Valdes, because he tended to sputter and his diction was bad. I got through the translation all right, with only one or two momentary hesitations, and then switched to the Polish-English line to hear how Gregori was doing with Janciewicz. Janciewicz was the cross Gregori had to bear, just as Valdes was mine.

Janciewicz repeated the previous remarks with a few ideological variations, and then the Secretary-General recognized the delegate from France, who introduced Dr. Denis Lévêque, the criminologist, and a great deal of complicated equipment was wheeled in.

Dr. Lévêque remarked that the question in many people's minds had been aptly expressed by the delegate from the U.S.S.R. at the preceding session, when he demanded, "What is the motive of the Kanamit? What is their purpose in offering us these unprecedented gifts, while asking nothing in return?"

The doctor then said, "At the request of several delegates and with the full consent of our guests, the Kanamit, my associates and I have made a series of tests upon the Kanamit with the equipment which you see before you. These tests will now be repeated."

A murmur ran through the chamber. There was a fusillade of flashbulbs, and one of the TV cameras moved up to focus on the instrument board of the doctor's equipment. At the same time, the huge television screen behind the podium lighted up, and we saw the blank faces of two dials, each with its pointer resting at zero, and a strip of paper tape with a stylus point resting against it.

The doctor's assistants were fastening wires to the temples of one of the Kanamit, wrapping a canvas-covered rubber tube around his forearm, and taping something to the palm of his right hand.

In the screen, we saw the paper tape begin to move while the stylus traced a slow zigzag pattern along it. One of the needles began to jump rhythmically; the other flipped over and stayed there, wavering slightly.

"These are the standard instruments for testing the truth of a statement," said Dr. Lévêque. "Our first object, since the physiology of the Kanamit is unknown to us, was to determine whether or not they react to these tests as human beings do. We will now repeat one of the many experiments which was made in the endeavor to discover this."

He pointed to the first dial. "This instrument registers the subject's heart-beat. This shows the electrical conductivity of the skin in the palm of his hand, a measure of perspiration, which increases under stress. And this"— pointing to the tape-and-stylus device—"shows the pattern and intensity of the electrical waves emanating from his brain. It has been shown, with human subjects, that all these readings vary markedly depending upon whether the subject is speaking the truth."

He picked up two large pieces of cardboard, one red and one black. The red one was a square about a meter on a side; the black was a rectangle a meter and a half long. He addressed himself to the Kanama:

"Which of these is longer than the other?"

"The red," said the Kanama.

Both needles leaped wildly, and so did the line on the unrolling tape.

"I shall repeat the question," said the doctor. "Which of these is longer than the other?"

"The black," said the creature.

This time the instruments continued in their normal rhythm.

"How did you come to this planet?" asked the doctor.

"Walked," replied the Kanama.

Again the instruments responded, and there was a subdued ripple of laughter in the chamber.

"Once more," said the doctor, "how did you come to this planet?"

"In a spaceship," said the Kanama, and the instruments did not jump.

The doctor again faced the delegates. "Many such experiments were made," he said, "and my colleagues and myself are satisfied that the mechanisms are effective. Now," he turned to the Kanama, "I shall ask our distinguished guest to reply to the question put at the last session by the delegate of the U.S.S.R., namely, what is the motive of the Kanamit people in offering these great gifts to the people of Earth?"

The Kanama rose. Speaking this time in English, he said, "On my planet there is a saying, 'There are more riddles in a stone than in a philosopher's head.' The motives of intelligent beings, though they may at times appear obscure, are simple things compared to the complex workings of the natural universe. Therefore I hope that the people of Earth will understand, and believe, when I tell you that our mission upon your planet is simply this—to bring to you the peace and plenty which we ourselves enjoy, and which we have in the past brought to other races throughout the galaxy. When your world has no more hunger, no more war, no more needless suffering, that will be our reward."

And the needles had not jumped once.

The delegate from the Ukraine jumped to his feet, asking to be recognized, but the time was up and the Secretary-General closed the session.

I met Gregori as we were leaving the U.N. chamber. His face was red with excitement. "Who promoted that circus?" he demanded.

"The tests looked genuine to me," I told him.

"A circus!" he said vehemently. "A second-rate farce! If they were genuine, Peter, why was debate stifled?"

"There'll be time for debate tomorrow surely."

"Tomorrow the doctor and his instruments will be back in Paris. Plenty of things can happen before tomorrow. In the name of sanity, man, how can anybody trust a thing that looks as if it ate the baby?"

I was a little annoyed. I said, "Are you sure you're not more worried about their politics than their appearance?"

He said, "Bah," and went away.

The next day reports began to come in from government laboratories all over the world where the Kanamit's power source was being tested. They were wildly enthusiastic. I don't understand such things myself, but it seemed that those little metal boxes would give more electrical power than an atomic pile, for next to nothing and nearly forever. And it was said that they were so cheap to manufacture that everybody in the world could have one of his own. In the early afternoon there were reports that seventeen countries had already begun to set up factories to turn them out.

The next day the Kanamit turned up with plans and specimens of a gadget that would increase the fertility of any arable land by sixty to one hundred per cent. It speeded the formation of nitrates in the soil, or something. There was nothing in the headlines but the Kanamit any more. The day after that, they dropped their bombshell.

"You now have potentially unlimited power and increased food supply," said one of them. He pointed with his three-fingered hand to an instrument that stood on the table before him. It was a box on a tripod, with a parabolic reflector on the front of it. "We offer you today a third gift which is at least as important as the first two."

He beckoned to the TV men to roll their cameras into closeup position. Then he picked up a large sheet of cardboard covered with drawings and English lettering. We saw it on the large screen above the podium; it was all clearly legible.

"We are informed that this broadcast is being relayed throughout your world," said the Kanama. "I wish that everyone who has equipment for taking photographs from television screens would use it now."

The Secretary-General leaned forward and asked a question sharply, but the Kanama ignored him.

"This device," he said, "projects a field in which no explosive, of whatever nature, can detonate."

There was an uncomprehending silence.

The Kanama said, "It cannot now be suppressed. If one nation has it, all must have it." When nobody seemed to understand, he explained bluntly, "There will be no more war."

That was the biggest news of the millennium, and it was perfectly true. It turned out that the explosives the Kanama was talking about included gasoline and Diesel explosions. They had simply made it impossible for anybody to mount or equip a modern army.

We could have gone back to bows and arrows, of course, but that wouldn't have satisfied the military. Not after having atomic bombs and all the rest. Besides, there wouldn't be any reason to make war. Every nation would soon have everything.

Nobody ever gave another thought to those lie-detector experiments, or asked the Kanamit what their politics were. Gregori was put out; he had nothing to prove his suspicions.

I quit my job with the U.N. a few months later, because I foresaw that it was going to die under me anyhow. U.N. business was booming at the time, but after a year or so there was going to be nothing for it to do. Every nation on Earth was well on the way to being completely self-supporting; they weren't going to need much arbitration.

I accepted a position as translator with the Kanamit Embassy, and it was there that I ran into Gregori again. I was glad to see him, but I couldn't imagine what he was doing there.

"I thought you were on the opposition," I said. "Don't tell me you're convinced the Kanamit are all right."

He looked rather shamefaced. "They're not what they look, anyhow," he said.

It was as much of a concession as he could decently make, and I invited him down to the embassy lounge for a drink. It was an intimate kind of place, and he grew confidential over the second daiquiri.

"They fascinate me," he said. "I hate them instinctively on sight still—that hasn't changed, but I can evaluate it. You were right, obviously; they mean us nothing but good. But do you know"—he leaned across the table —"the question of the Soviet delegate was never answered."

I am afraid I snorted.

"No, really," he said. "They told us what they wanted to do—'to bring to you the peace and plenty which we ourselves enjoy.' But they didn't say *why*."

"Why do missionaries—"

"Hogwash!" he said angrily. "Missionaries have a religious motive. If these creatures have a religion, they haven't once mentioned it. What's more, they didn't send a missionary group, they sent a diplomatic delegation—a group representing the will and policy of their whole people. Now just what have the Kanamit, as a people or a nation, got to gain from our welfare?"

I said, "Cultural—"

"Cultural cabbage-soup! No, it's something less obvious than that, something obscure that belongs to their psychology and not to ours. But trust me, Peter, there is no such thing as a completely disinterested altruism. In one way or another, they have something to gain."

"And that's why you're here," I said, "to try to find out what it is?"

"Correct. I wanted to get on one of the ten-year exchange groups to their home planet, but I couldn't; the quota was filled a week after they made the announcement. This is the next best thing. I'm studying their language, and you know that language reflects the basic assumptions of the people who use it. I've got a fair command of the spoken lingo already. It's not hard, really, and there are hints in it. Some of the idioms are quite similar to English. I'm sure I'll get the answer eventually."

"More power," I said, and we went back to work.

I saw Gregori frequently from then on, and he kept me posted about his progress. He was highly excited about a month after that first meeting; said he'd got hold of a book of the Kanamit's and was trying to puzzle it out. They wrote in ideographs, worse than Chinese, but he was determined to fathom it if it took him years. He wanted my help.

Well, I was interested in spite of myself, for I knew it would be a long job. We spent some evenings together, working with material from Kanamit bulletin-boards and so forth, and the extremely limited English-Kanamit dictionary they issued the staff. My conscience bothered me about the stolen book, but gradually I became absorbed by the problem. Languages are my field, after all. I couldn't help being fascinated.

We got the title worked out in a few weeks. It was

"How to Serve Man," evidently a handbook they were giving out to new Kanamit members of the embassy staff. They had new ones in, all the time now, a shipload about once a month; they were opening all kinds of research laboratories, clinics and so on. If there was anybody on Earth besides Gregori who still distrusted those people, he must have been somewhere in the middle of Tibet.

It was astonishing to see the changes that had been wrought in less than a year. There were no more standing armies, no more shortages, no unemployment. When you picked up a newspaper you didn't see "H-BOMB" or "V-2" leaping out at you; the news was always good. It was a hard thing to get used to. The Kanamit were working on human biochemistry, and it was known around the embassy that they were nearly ready to announce methods of making our race taller and stronger and healthier— practically a race of supermen—and they had a potential cure for heart disease and cancer.

I didn't see Gregori for a fortnight after we finished working out the title of the book; I was on a long-overdue vacation in Canada. When I got back, I was shocked by the change in his appearance.

"What on earth is wrong, Gregori?" I asked. "You look like the very devil."

"Come down to the lounge."

I went with him, and he gulped a stiff Scotch as if he needed it.

"Come on, man, what's the matter?" I urged.

"The Kanamit have put me on the passenger list for the next exchange ship," he said. "You, too, otherwise I wouldn't be talking to you."

"Well," I said, "but—"

"They're not altruists."

I tried to reason with him. I pointed out they'd made Earth a paradise compared to what it was before. He only shook his head.

Then I said, "Well, what about those lie-detector tests?"

"A farce," he replied, without heat. "I said so at the time, you fool. They told the truth, though, as far as it went."

"And the book?" I demanded, annoyed. "What about that—'How to Serve Man'? That wasn't put there for you to read. They *mean* it. How do you explain that?"

"I've read the first paragraph of that book," he said. "Why do you suppose I haven't slept for a week?"

I said, "Well?" and he smiled a curious, twisted smile. "It's a cookbook," he said.

THE BOMB IN THE BATHTUB

THOMAS N. SCORTIA

THE YOUNG MAN SAID HIS NAME WAS SIDNEY COLEMAN. He looked rather like a smooth-muscled distance swimmer, lately taken to fat. At the moment, his eyes were sunken and wild-looking.

"He said my bathroom was the center of a probability nexus," the young man wailed. "And now there's an H-bomb in my bathtub."

Caedman Wickes rubbed a lean red hand across the scarred surface of his desk and winced at the gritty feel of dust under his palm.

Then he closely inspected the coarse blond bristles on the backs of his fingers.

"Does it do anything else?" he asked at last with great deliberation. "Tick, for instance?"

"Nothing. It just lies there, eying the hot water faucet with that stupid blue eye and mouthing all sorts of platitudes."

"Isn't this all a little ridiculous?" Wickes asked.

"That's what the police thought." Coleman ran blunt fingers through close-cropped black hair.

"No, I didn't mean that. After all," Wickes pointed out, "if you're going to put anything as big as a bomb in the bathroom, the logical place is the bathtub."

"Logical to you, maybe."

Wickes touched his nose reflectively and gestured toward the office door. Its chipped markings spelled in mirrored reverse: *Caedman Wickes, Private Investigator, Specializing in Odd Complaints.*

He said, "In my business, I often encounter the unusual. But there's always an internal logic. That's the guiding principle of my success. Always—*always* look for the internal logic. All else follows."

He steepled his fingers reminiscently. "I remember a client who thought he had a Venusian trapped in his washing machine. Very logical, if you stop to think about it. However—" Wickes pursed his lips sorrowfully, "it developed that he was quite mad. A pity, too. Such a lovely idea. Anyway, I meant the idea of using an H-bomb was ridiculous. The best that such a bomb could do would be to vaporize the city and possibly the nearer suburbs. Hardly worth worrying about."

"He didn't actually say it was an H-bomb," Coleman said tiredly. "I just assumed that's what it was. After all, he did say he wanted to destroy this universe."

"Ah!" Wickes's eyes gleamed. "Not the Universe? Just *this* universe?"

"He made a point of that. He said there are an infinite number of probable universes. He just wants to destroy the best of all possible universes—*this* one."

"Undoubtedly paranoid," Wickes commented.

"Of course. This is part of his therapy. He's insane."

"Then this isn't his universe?"

"I should think not. The cure wouldn't be of much use if he destroyed the universe in which he exists, would it?"

Wickes pursed his lips. "That doesn't necessarily follow. Why, I remember—"

Coleman leaped to his feet and leaned forward, bracing his hands on the desk. "Don't! I've had enough of your wool-gathering. That thing says it's going to detonate this Tuesday. You've got to figure a way to defuse it."

"Patience, patience," Wickes chided. "It never pays to lose one's head about these things."

He unfolded his cadaverous six-foot-seven frame from behind the desk, secured a trenchcoat, black wool scarf and stained snap-brim felt hat from the top of a battered filing cabinet.

"I really should smoke a pipe," he mused as he donned the garments, "but I do think the coat and hat are enough of a concession to convention, don't you?"

"I don't give a damn if you wear pink tights and fly

through the air," Coleman snorted. "Just do something about that bomb in my bathtub."

Wickes gestured limply toward the door.

"I can see," he said as they walked through the hall, their feet evoking protesting squeaks from the curling boards of the floor, "that you don't appreciate the essential beauty of the situation."

"Beauty? How would you like a bomb in *your* bathtub?"

"Not the point at all," Wickes reproved. "Now this much reminds me of the client who had a scheme to psychoanalyze his great-great-great-grandfather. Had a theory that neuroses were transmitted genetically. Well, he wanted me to ascertain the old gentleman's whereabouts on a certain day in the early eighteen-thirties and—"

Coleman was looking wildly to the right and left as they descended the stairs. Wickes decided to ignore his distress. Besides, the Adventure of the Retroactive Psychoanalysis, as he was fond of calling it, helped him develop the proper mood.

He was a little annoyed, as they shared a taxi crosstown, that Coleman displayed such a lamentable lack of interest in bearing his proper share of the conversation. He fidgeted continually and evidenced a tendency to start at any loud noise. Once, when an auto backfired, he almost collapsed.

No resiliency, Wickes thought, and clicked his tongue mentally.

The house was a small five-room contemporary in one of the newer developments on the fringe of the city.

As Coleman unlocked the front door, Wickes stood looking up and down the block.

"Odd," he said.

"What's that?"

"No television antennae."

"You won't find any in this area," Coleman explained. "We're in a dead spot. Not even radio reception. That's why I got the house so cheaply."

As they entered the house, Wickes became aware of a thin atonal humming in the air. It had an odd musical quality without actually approaching melody.

"Oh, I forgot to tell you," Coleman said. "It sings."

Wickes raised an eyebrow. "The bomb sings? In the bathtub?"

"In the bathtub."

"How appropriate," Wickes said.

While Coleman removed his hat and coat, Wickes crossed the living room, following the sound through a short hall to a large bathroom, done in shades of coral and rose.

There was quite a large bomb in the bathtub.

It had a single vacant-looking blue eye. It was staring at the hot water faucet and singing.

"You see?" Coleman said from behind him. "The police wouldn't believe me." His voice was shrill and hysterical.

"This is the best of all possible worlds," the bomb said. "But tomorrow will be better."

"Interesting," Wickes said.

"What am I going to do?" Coleman wailed.

"Every day, in every way, things are getting better

and better," the bomb intoned. Its humming rose in pitch a fraction of an octave.

"Incurable optimist," Wickes observed.

"You!" Coleman sobbed. "Get out of my bathtub!"

"Can't," the bomb said, interrupting its singing. "No legs. No arms. I won't," it added after a moment.

It started to sing again. The music was oddly regular, with an internal consistency that Wickes found vaguely familiar.

"What are you singing?" he asked.

" 'Frankie and Johnnie'," the bomb said. For the first time, the blue eye moved from the faucet to stare at Wickes. "Like it?"

"Well," Wickes said, considering, "it doesn't sound much like 'Frankie and Johnnie'."

"It is, though," the bomb said. "I'm coding it."

"It's giving me a headache," Coleman complained.

"Philistine," the bomb sneered, but the singing rose in pitch and quickly became inaudible. The eye returned to its fixed stare. This time, it chose the cold water faucet.

"You'd better lie down," Wickes advised Coleman.

He pulled a tape measure from his pocket and began to measure the relationship of the fixtures in the bathroom to each other. Occasionally he clicked his tongue and made quick notes in a brown leatherette notebook.

Coleman watched him silently.

The bomb continued its idiot stare at the water faucet.

Wickes mumbled something.

"What's that?" Coleman asked.

"Like Count Buffon's needle problem," Wickes said. "The ratio of the bathtub width to the width of the room."

"What about it?"

"Three point one four one six," Wickes intoned. "Pi, that is."

He nodded and pushed the bathmat up against the stool. Thoughtfully, he produced a pair of dice from his pocket. He began to roll them on the floor, bouncing them against the tiled base of the tub.

The dice repeatedly came up seven.

"My advice," Wickes said slowly.

"Yes?" Coleman urged.

"When this is all over—"

"Yes?"

"—I'd tear out the bathtub and install a dice table. Of course, you'd have to change the house rules somewhat, since each throw would be a seven, but—"

He was speaking to an empty doorway. Coleman had stumbled weakly down the hall to collapse in a chair in the living room. From the bathroom, Wickes heard him groan softly.

"This is the best of all possible worlds," the bomb said in a dogmatic tone.

"Is it?" Wickes asked.

"Oh, yes indeed. It has to be. Betcha," it challenged smugly. Then it began to sing again.

"Can't you sing anything but 'Frankie and Johnnie'?" Wickes asked.

"That was 'Down by the Old Mill Stream'."

"It sounded like 'Frankie and Johnnie'."

"No breeding," the bomb sniffed. "This is undoubtedly the best of all possible worlds," it added after a moment.

"Why?" Wickes demanded.

"Oh, it just is."

"That's not true, you know. Actually, it's a pretty inferior world."

"It is not! It *has* to be the best!"

"I'm afraid it's not."

"Lies, lies!" the bomb exclaimed passionately. "I'll give you odds—any odds."

"You mean bet?"

"Of course! Afraid?"

"Why does it have to be the best of possible worlds?"

"Put up or shut up."

"Why the best of possible worlds?" Wickes insisted.

The bomb was silent. Then it began to hum in a rising crescendo. Wickes walked to the living room. Coleman was sitting in a chair, his head in his hands.

" 'Frankie and Johnnie'?" he asked wanly.

" 'Down by the Old Mill Stream'," Wickes told him.

" 'Mairzy Doats'," the bomb corrected from the bathroom.

"You know," Wickes said, "this could get quite maddening."

"Why didn't you take the bet?" Coleman asked sarcastically.

"No need to be snide. Besides, I never bet. Still, that bit is significant."

"How so?"

"Well, you can infer certain things about a society whose machines like to gamble."

"Yeah," Coleman said. "Maybe that universe has been conquered by a race of one-armed bandits from Las Vegas."

"Not in the least unlikely," Wickes said. "Except that this one has no arms. Anyway, the world of the bomb certainly knows more about probability than we do."

" 'Find the internal logic?' " Coleman quoted.

"Exactly," Wickes said, with surprised approval. "I couldn't have put it more succinctly myself."

Wickes seated himself in a barrel chair and looked fixedly at the tips of his black shoes. Finally, he rose and walked to the phone on the table by Coleman's chair.

"It's about time," Coleman remarked acidly.

"Tush," Wickes said.

He dialed a number and spoke for a few moments. Then he dialed another number. After a short, low conversation, he replaced the phone triumphantly.

"Hah," he said.

"Hah?" Coleman queried. "Hah?"

"Yes, hah. That was the program director of WWVI. They have a disk jockey on now."

"With a bomb ready to explode," Coleman cried, "he phones requests to disk jockeys. What did you ask for? 'Mairzy Doats'?"

"That wasn't necessary. They've just played it. And before that, 'Down by the Old Mill Stream'. And before that—"

" 'Frankie and Johnnie'?"

"Precisely. I see you understand my methods."

"Yes," Coleman said weakly and sank back into his chair.

"Now I must leave," Wickes said.

"With that still in there? What about me?"

"Well, you could read to it," Wickes suggested.

Coleman stared as Wickes walked to a bookcase by the door and scanned the titles. He selected a book and handed it to Coleman.

"This," he said.

"*Crime and Punishment?*"

"A delightful book," Wickes said. "So full of—of—" He waved his hand uncertainly. "Of *weltschmerz*. Oh, yes," he said at the door. "If you get bored with that, try *The Seven Who Were Hanged*. A little healthy morbidity will do worlds of good—even for a bomb."

And he closed the door with appropriate consideration.

After leaving Coleman, Wickes walked for several blocks, lost in thought. The situation, he decided, did have its intriguing points. The particular problem was the point of contact. Obviously nothing would be gained by merely defusing the bomb. The alien organization of therapists who had placed it there would merely try again, perhaps with more success.

But how to move against those unpredictable minds in the unguessable gamble? Rather like the great-to-the-fourth-power-grandfather acting against Wickes's own psychoanalysis-bent client.

The lever—if only there were some lever. But there was only the bomb with its insane optimism and wild gambling fever and equally insane habit of encoding popular songs.

He stopped in the middle of the sidewalk, heedless of the glares of passersby. In seconds, his head was wreathed in a thick tobacco smoke of concentration. He became aware of his surroundings again only when the pipe stem grew too hot.

He hailed a cab and gave directions to the local branch library. There he spent some time among the math shelves, selecting first one volume on statistics and probability and then another. Finally he found what he wanted, a long table of random numbers used in setting up random sequences in physical experiments. When the librarian wasn't looking, he stealthily tore out the two pages of the table and left.

Then he went to a magic store, where he bought a deck of marked cards, a pair of trick dice and a book on roulette systems. In the taxi, he read through the opening chapters of the roulette book and finally tossed it from the window when the cab stopped for a red light.

At his office, he made two phone calls, one to a friend who was an electronics engineer, the other to a friend who played the bassoon. Then he scrambled beneath his filing cabinet until he found a battered tape recorder that he used as a dictaphone, drew on the trenchcoat and battered hat, and headed for the street.

After spending three hours with his bassoon-playing friend, he dropped by his engineer-friend's house to pick up the pieces of equipment that his friend had assembled for him. He stopped at a drugstore for a quick snack and arrived at Coleman's house at seven-forty.

"It's about time," the young man said. "I'm absolutely hoarse." He was carrying the copy of *Crime and Punishment*, his thumb inserted in a place about a third of the way through. As he closed the door, Wickes heard a faint muttering from the bathroom.

"Lies, lies," the bomb was saying.

"It doesn't like Dostoievsky," Coleman sighed.

"*De gustibus non est disputandum*," Wickes airily explained.

"Yeah," Coleman said uncertainly.

"I," Wickes announced grandly as he removed his coat with a flourish, "have been learning to compose for the bassoon."

He gestured toward the peeling leather case of the tape recorder, which he had placed next to a featureless black suitcase.

Coleman stared at him with lips compressed.

"Oh, hand me my coat a minute," Wickes said. "That's a good fellow."

He extracted several rolled newspapers, which he proceeded to unroll. Several items on the front pages were outlined in black.

"Dostoievsky is all very well," Wickes said, "but we mustn't neglect current events." He smirked knowingly.

Coleman's lips became even whiter.

"Here," Wickes said, handing Coleman a small package.

"What is it?" Coleman asked hopefully.

"Dice. We may want to get up a crap game."

"Have you gone—"

"Mad? Oh, no. At least, not in the usual sense. Now let me see how this operates."

"This" was the enigmatic black suitcase from which Wickes extracted a bewildering assortment of electronic parts. Following a diagram he took from his pocket, he began to connect the several units together. Eventually, he ran a long wire across the room, hanging it over the doorway and the living room drapes.

"Antenna," he explained.

He found a wall plug and connected the device. Then he began to assemble the tape recorder.

"Wait till you hear this," he said. "Bassoon solo."

"The man has gone batty," Coleman glumly told the walls.

Wickes twisted several dials on the recorder and flipped a toggle on the other device. The room suddenly filled with the low-register grunts of a bassoon. The notes were long and anguished and made absolutely no melody.

Coleman slapped his hands to his ears as the discordance was echoed by a sudden blast of sound from the bathroom.

"You see," Wickes yelled above the maddening cacophony, "the bomb is in constant communication with its makers. It uses the radio waves that are absorbed in this dead space. That's why you can't get reception in this area. A natural consequence of the probability nexus in the bathroom is to shunt all radiation into the universe from which the bomb comes."

"Yes, but—"

"So we feed it random radio impulses—my bassoon solo composed from a table of random numbers. It can't code a random sequence. Ergo, it can't communicate."

At this point, the bomb made a loud groaning noise.

"Now!" Wickes cried with a wild gleam in his eyes. He charged for the bathroom, a rolled newspaper outthrust before him like a lance.

The bomb lay in the bathtub, moaning softly. Coleman halted behind Wickes as he held up the newspaper and began to read.

" 'Father Slays Family of Five,' " Wickes intoned.

The quivering bomb screamed piercingly.

" 'Thousands Die in Wake of Eruption,' " he read.

"Lies, lies, lies, lies!"

" 'Indian Plague Takes Million Lives.' "

The bomb began to howl, its voice rising to an ear-splitting pitch.

"Here! You stop that!"

Wickes turned to the gleaming machine that occupied the space where one wall of the bathroom had been.

"I said stop that," the bald little man in the machine said.

"It's him, it's him," Coleman bleated. "The man I told you about when I came to your office."

"Interesting," Wickes said. He pointed toward the machine's lower quarter, where a small metallic sign glowed. The sign said: "Paranoids Anonymous. 'You, too, can destroy a universe.' "

"Stop it, I say!" the little man yelled, waving what was obviously a weapon.

"Turn off the tape recorder," Wickes told Coleman. Coleman headed toward the living room.

"What's the big idea?" the man demanded as he descended from the machine. His face was stormy under thick brows. He was dressed in a pair of shorts and singlet tailored from some metallic material. Calf-length boots encased his feet. A harness of some type encircled his waist and shoulders, and from this harness, various unknown pieces of apparatus dangled.

"This is the best of all possible worlds," the bomb said with the suspicion of a sniffle.

"Of course it is," the man said soothingly. "Don't you let anyone tell you it isn't."

"Any odds it isn't?" Wickes offered.

"Huh!" the man said. But he looked interested.

"Afraid of losing your—ah—shirt?" Wickes demanded.

"Won't do you any good," the man said darkly. "Got to destroy a universe. The best one. This is it."

A small box that depended from the harness buzzed softly. The man removed it, pressed it to his lips and spoke a few incomprehensible words.

"Look," Wickes said, "this has to be the best of all possible universes, doesn't it?"

"It is," the man said smugly. "They planned it that way."

"They?"

"My psychometricians. It wouldn't do to destroy just any universe. It has to be the best."

"I must say you're remarkably objective about it."

"Why not? It's *my* neurosis, isn't it?"

"Maybe this isn't the best of all possible worlds."

"Ridiculous," mumbled the bomb from the bathtub.

"Best for whom?" Wickes demanded. "By whose standards? Yours?"

"Naturally."

"Want to bet?"

The man licked his lips. "Nobody ever accused me of being a con."

"If it's the best possible world for you," Wickes said, "you should win."

"True, true," said the bomb.

Coleman had returned to the room. He was eying the bald little man with something akin to horror.

"The dice, please," Wickes said to Coleman.

"What's the idea?" the man demanded.

"I'll prove my point."

The bald man smiled shrewdly. "There's something you should know."

"Never mind."

"Don't say I didn't try to warn you."

"Let's make this interesting," Wickes said. "A little side bet?"

"Done." The man pulled filmy currency from one pocket.

"I can't spend your money," Wickes pointed out.

"You can't win anyway."

"How about something more tangible?" Wickes asked. "One of those gadgets, for instance." He pointed to the harness.

"Roll them from the wall," the man said, extracting one of the instruments.

Wickes sank to one knee and rolled the dice. They came up double fours.

"Hah!" Wickes said.

He rolled three more times. On the fourth roll, the dice came up six and two.

Half an hour later, Wickes had stripped the visitor to his shorts.

The man jumped angrily to his feet. "You switched dice!"

"Prove it."

"I quit."

"Coward! I mean con!"

"That does it. You!" The man yelled at the bomb. "Forget about Tuesday! Detonate in one hour!"

Then he leaped into the machine and it flickered from view.

"Now you've done it," Coleman moaned.

"Today is the finest day of all," the bomb said.

"Hm-m-m," Wickes mused, inspecting the pile of loot at his feet. Finally he selected the box-like communicator that the man had used and inspected it closely.

Coleman sank to the floor and began to roll the abandoned dice dispiritedly. After a moment, he picked them up and examined them closely.

"Hey!" he exclaimed. "These dice don't have any ones, threes or fives!"

"That's right," Wickes said.

"Then how can you throw sevens?"

"You can't."

"But that's dishonest."

"Why? He was trying to cheat me."

As Coleman pondered the question, Wickes began to speak earnestly into the communicator. Before long, he seemed satisfied.

"Well, now," he said, "let's relax. Can you make some coffee?"

"That thing is ready to go off in an hour," Coleman protested. "Do something!"

"Patience, patience. All that can be done has been done."

He walked down the hall to the living room, Coleman trailing him dejectedly.

"At least call the bomb squad," Coleman said.

"Hardly necessary."

"You blasted crackpot!"

"There's no need to be abusive," Wickes said. "If you'll only apply logic, you'll see that certain features of this other universe may be—"

"Peace, my children," said a voice from the bathroom.

Standing in the doorway was the majestic figure of a man. He was tall and very fair, with a light crown of blond hair. His eyes were expressive and ethereal.

"Well," Wickes said, "you certainly didn't waste time."

"I am always ready for a suffering universe," the man said, lifting his eyes unto the ceiling.

"It's in the bathroom," Wickes said.

"I have already taken care of it," the man replied, "while you two were having your childish tiff."

"Childish!" Coleman cried. "If you think—"

"Peace, brotherhood," the man said. "We must all live in perfect love."

He turned and walked back toward the bathroom.

"Wait," Wickes called and hurried after him. Coleman followed awkwardly, his eyes wide and unbelieving. In the bathroom, the tub was quite empty.

"Love is all-powerful," the saintlike man said. For the first time, Wickes noticed the faint halo flickering above his head.

The man began to mount a machine in the wall.

"Alas," he sighed, "other worlds, other needs. Busy, busy."

Before the machine flickered from sight, Wickes saw the flickering metal sign on the machine.

It said: "Messiahs, Incorporated. 'You, too, can save a universe.'"

Later, in the living room, Coleman sprawled limply on the divan while Wickes leaned on the mantel and stared dreamily into the dead fireplace, sucking on his unlit pipe.

"I can see how you cut off the bomb's communication," Coleman said, "but why the newspapers?"

"Well," Wickes explained, "it wouldn't have done our paranoid friend to destroy just any universe. It couldn't be one that was better off obliterated or there would be no point to the therapy. Hence Dostoievsky and the newspapers. I had to demonstrate the world was better off destroyed. That's the only way I could pry the paranoid from his vantage point in his world. Destroy the bomb's conviction that this was the best universe, but prevent the bomb's getting the complete story back to him."

"But that rigged crap game?"

"Well, it was obvious that they set great store by gambling. Moreover, I was certain the box he used kept him in contact with his world. I had only to win the communicator. All else followed."

"By internal logic?"

"Of course."

"Like Venusians in washing machines."

"Naturally."

"Forgive me for being stupid," Coleman said ironically.

"You're just not used to thinking in these terms," Wickes said. "Surely it must be obvious that if there is an organization that aids paranoids by allowing them to destroy a universe, there must be some counter-organization for those poor fellows who want to save a universe."

"Messiahs, Incorporated?"

"Exactly. The internal logic of the situation demanded it. I had only to contact them. The job was made to order —a universe that needed saving."

Coleman struggled to his feet. "I think I need an aspirin," he said weakly. He stumbled down the hall to the bathroom.

Wickes heard his sudden cry of alarm. He ran toward the bathroom. Coleman had collapsed into the bathtub.

The little man in the scarlet-edged toga was waving

a dagger wildly. He stopped when he saw Wickes and smiled apologetically.

"Oh, my," he said. "You *aren't* Julius Caesar, are you?"

He moved swiftly toward his machine in the wall.

Before it disappeared, Wickes managed to decipher the flickering sign on its frame.

It read: "Hindsight, Unlimited. 'You, too, can change a universe.' "

Wickes clasped his hands together ecstatically.

"Lovely," he murmured. "Simply lovely."

In the bathtub, Coleman only whimpered.

THE BLACK SORCERER OF THE BLACK CASTLE
ANDREW J BLACK-OFFUTT

KIMON THE KONERIAN GAZED UP AT THE BLACK CASTLE towering into the moonless sky, its murky turrets and minarets resembling dark fingers pointing the way to the shadow gods. Kimon chuckled, the deep-throated sound of a giant of a man from a dark barbarian land. Well, he mused, soon the black magician Reh and all his daemonic guardians would go to meet those sombre gods of Atramentos—or he himself would. He loosened the black pommel of his long sword, Goreater, glanced at the ring on his finger, and mounted the hill to the castle.

A small man named Kohl had told him of the place. In the Black Castle of Atramentos, Kohl had said, lay the

Princess Sabell, captive of the sorcerer Reh. The keep was rendered impregnable by Reh's spells and his daemons. The princess alone knew the whereabouts of the jewels of Chthon: gems worth the ransom of King Minaceos himself. A man did not go about rescuing princesses without reason! Over cups of wine in a dim tavern, the two men agreed to share the treasure. Then, because one was a barbarian and such men are well known to have codes, and to rely on muscle and might rather than shrewd double-dealing, Kohl told Kimon how to reach the place. He told, too, of the power of the ring he wore; while it made no magic, it negated all spells cast against the wearer.

They rose and departed, Kohl leading the way. In the dark street he said, over his shoulder, "Few men would I trust behind me with the knowledge I have imparted to you, O Kimon. But 'tis well known that ye barbars are men of great honour, not backstabbers, and—" Which was when Kimon, reminded that Kohl was no longer necessary, stabbed him in the back. He took the ring, of course, before slinging the man into the inkiness of an alley.

After walking a block he had hurried back to take Kohl's purse.

Now, gazing up at the castle, Kimon chuckled. Where had the poor idiot gotten such idiot notions of honour among barbars? Shaking his head, he set his foot on the hill on which stood the umbrageous castle.

The monster bird came winging down like a great storm cloud heavy with rain, its leathery wings flapping with the sound of thunder. It paused above his head, steadying itself on wings the size of a trireme's sail, then folded them to careen down at him. Its awesome cry filled the air rent by its passage: "Kamikaze!"

Goreater ate.

Clapping a hand over the inch-deep scratches laying bare the sheaves of muscle in his mighty chest, Kimon looked down at the crumpled body of the bird. It writhed even in death, some awful virescent ichor bubbling from its neck. Then it vanished.

Kimon went on, paying little heed to the six-inch-long wounds in his chest; they were relatively inconsequential and would heal in a month or three. Besides, the trickling blood warmed his bare flesh. As he drew nigher he began to feel the strangeness of the place, the evil. Trailing tendrils of wraithy stuff like cobwebs seemed to writhe over his visage. He blinked and shook his head, raising his hands to tear his way clear. But his fingers touched nothing. His eyes saw nothing. There was nothing there; no cobwebs, no tendrils, no cobs, merely the eerie feel of them. He shivered. Neither man nor beast had been woman-spawned to strike fear in the big barbarian's heart. But this palpable evil born of warlocks and shades, the shadow-world of necromancy and spectres, that otherworld of apparitions and divinations and things a man could feel but not see . . . these brought a shiver to Kimon and set his teeth a-rattle in his head. He touched the ring, realising that he had fought and slain a sorcerer's daemon with nought but his own thews and sword.

But now fear laid nordic fingers upon him, tightened them about his heart. Again he shivered. He began to shake. He felt hot water and an atrabilious taste in his mouth and turned away, whimpering, to flee.

Then, knees shaking, hands chill and wet, he realised what was taking place. He mouthed a foul barbaric oath despite the sorcerous fear attacking him. As if rooted in quicksand, he turned slowly, slowly to face the castle. Raising his left hand, he aimed the ring at those misty towers.

"I defy you!" he bellowed, and thrice he repeated those words that Kohl had taught him carefully, with but a half-hour of rehearsal. And the ring seemed to come alive, to glow and shimmer and pour strength down his arm.

The mists vanished. The ghostwebs ceased their invisible twisting. His fear left him. And there before him stood—the black castle of Atramentos! No longer was it a shadowy thing of fear and unholy blackness; now it was merely a towering pile of blackest basalt, gleaming liquidly even in the moonless night. The door rose before him, twice his height. A chain with links as big as his thumbs was looped through the handle, secured to great spikes on either side.

Growling low in his throat, Kimon drew Goreater. He sucked in a mighty breath and, laying hold of the pommel with both hands, swung the glaive far back over his shoulder to bring it whistling down with all the strength of his corded muscles. Sparks flew as he smote the chain. Shock blazed up his arms like tongues of lightning. The rebounding sword nearly took off his head.

Rattling, the chain held.

Then he noticed. It was merely looped over the spike on the left. "Spit!" Sheepishly he reached up to pull it off and thread it through the handle. He placed one foot against the door and shoved. It swung in, strangely, without creaking. An odour of death, of mouldering earth housing mouldering corpses, rushed out to greet him with chill embrace. With Goreater ready in his hand, he entered the murkiness of the hall.

The serpent was upon him before he knew of its existence. Its shimmering scales rose above him, its xanthic eyes gazing at him like the very fires of blackest Hades. Far behind him he could see its immense body stretching off along the hallway. He sniffed the evil odour of its breath as it hissed, felt the blast of fetid air, and hurled himself aside as the eyes blazed up, like the coals of a stirred fire, to shoot forward at him.

Kimon moved with a swiftness greater even than the reptile's. The great head swished past. Goreater swished after it. The monster body shivered and lashed in the final torment of death as the head plopped to the floor and rolled away. It exuded a vast pool of nigrescent ichor. The last lash of the terrible tail caught Kimon just below the knees and sent him flying through the air to sprawl in a great room beyond the hall. He rolled, somehow clinging to Goreater.

And good it was that Kimon did.

"Black devils of Lincar!" he muttered, and got to his feet, crouching; fortunately he had been knocked only thirty or forty feet and was unhurt but for a few cracked ribs. He straightened a broken finger with a swift jerk, glancing about. Here there was light, and as he glanced down, the body of that megatherian reptile vanished. But his perils were not at an end.

Approaching him now were men that were not men,

alive yet not alive—creatures dead but not dead. Full half a score of them there were, bearing the gaping wounds that had been the violent death of them. The eyes of one were popped wide and his black tongue lolled forth as it had at the moment he had been slain by the reptile in some darkling yesterday. They advanced, creatures returned to ghostly life by Reh's evil spells, and Kimon saw himself mirrored in them. These were his predecessors; would-be heroes who had come here in times past on the same mission as he. Clawed hands rose as they advanced jerkily upon him.

The first Kimon met with flashing sword to send his arm flopping away across the floor, black blood spattering forth. The fingers still clutched and flexed. The shriek ripped from the creature's throat chilled Kimon's very blood. The howl and the gore told him, though, that dead these men might be, but alive they were, too, and killed they could. Be. He hurled the thing aside, the scarlet stump of its arm still pumping out its pseudo life.

Then Goreater was a flashing, live thing, spattering walls and ceiling and floor with the steaming crimson wake of its terrible smiting passage. A black giant from Minatoa he ran through and through and yanked free his sword, feeling the dying man's claw tear his arm as he fell. A smallish fellow Kimon seized and swung up to grip by his heels, then swung him in an arc that downed one, two, three of the others. Then he released the fellow and heard the dropped-melon noise as his skull burst against the wall to spew forth rank red blood and gray brainstuff. Whilst the others shrank back, checked by their awe, Kimon moved as the wolf descends upon chicks. He struck the heads from three men he had downed.

Kimon's dread battle cry ripped from his lips as he spun to the man whose arm he had lopped off: "WHEEE-EEEEEEEEE!" he shouted, and the fellow's head leapt to join his arm on the gore-slippery floor. He turned in time to dodge a great ax in the hands of a fellow whose face was one hideous wound. He had been killed in some bygone time by the monster bird outside. Kimon's foot swept up to complete the destruction of that poor once-face, crushing nose and teeth and bursting eyeballs from their sockets to sail like agates into the air—and splitting open several of Kimon's toes, as he was wearing sandals. Blood bathed his legs and toes.

But four remained now, and Kimon roared at them to come join their comrades. They came. They were mindless *things*, restored but temporarily from the dead to serve as fighting machines for the master of this castle of horror. The cry of the maimed and the dying was in Kimon's ears and his veins, and his own battle cry joined them to spur him forward. Reason decamped.

They fell, gushing forth their carmine juices, their souls leaping forth to meet their liberator, the ever-hungry Goreater. And Goreater ate, and drank as well, and once again dead men died. The musty halls of that darkling castle reeked and smoked with blood and gore, rang with the fearsome cry of the big barbar from the mountains of Koneria and with the dying cries of those sent to destroy him.

And then he stood alone, nostrils flaring, for he had

slain many, and was very nearly winded. All about him lay corpses and hands and limbs no longer joined one to the other. His feet were planted in curdling blood and his toes smarted. Deliberately he tore loose the ripped flesh from his arm, for it bothered him as he hacked the heads from those not already beheaded. In the event he failed, Reh would no longer use these men who should long ago have been walking with the shades in the afterworld. He stood there, his own blood and theirs streaming and dripping from him, and he looked about.

"REH!—blackest creature on the earth's scarred face! —resurrector of slain men! Reh, commander of the legions of Hades! Your oversized sparrow died outside, your swollen fishing worm in the hall! And at my feet lie ten heads lonely for their decomposing bodies! What ELSE would you send to meet Kimon of Koneria?"

His voice rang down empty halls, dashed into dark empty rooms and out again, rose up the long stairway before him, shouted back at him from shroud-draped walls of black basalt. And he waited, and there was no answer. Again he filled his lungs to roar out his challenge, again he flung wide his jaws to shout. Then, at the head of the steps, there stood Reh, Black Sorcerer of the Black Castle of Atramentos. Actually he was very pale.

His eyes blazed down at Kimon as had the dead serpent's. A slender nose arced out between them, hooked like the beak of the prodigious bird. Below that nose writhed tendrils of a black moustache like the wraithy fear-tendrils that had caressed Kimon outside the warlock's lair. And below the moustache was a lipless slash of a mouth, resembling nothing more than the old wounds of the dead men at Kimon's feet.

Below that, of course, Reh wore the official uniform of the Sorcerers, Fiends, and Warlocks Association, a loose-sleeved black robe.

"Kimon of Koneria, is it? And you have destroyed my guardians and penetrated to the very marrow of my keep! Well, Kimon, well-met! Join me here, mightiest of men, that I need fear no more intruders. Be the guardian of the Black Castle!"

Kimon's eyes were like the bubbling tar pits of Nigressa as he stared back at the thaumaturge. "Join you, hell-creaure? Live here, as guardian of this tomb? I love life too much to live here with DEATH! You've *got* to be KIDDING!"

Reh's drooping moustaches wriggled like tentacles as his mouth pretended to smile. He waved his hand, tracing invisible patterns in the air. And the air was filled with the golden light of a thousand candles; the birdsongs of lutes and belly-booms of drums and the undulating skirl of pipes. A vision rose up to fill the room before Kimon's eyes: a vision of the finest of succulent viands and the richest wines served in aureate goblets; of pillows of the softest fabrics and hues. And there were women: slender girls with breasts round and cupped as goblets; eyes telling of love and desire, hips churning and yearning toward him. And there were others, too, more to the liking of a bronzed barbarian; deep-chested women with holes of navels winking in their round bellies and arms to crush a man in hot embrace. Their eyes were for him and him alone, their forms coppery chalices of sensuality. Kimon saw, and stared, and his great sword was forgotten in a lifeless hand as he started toward them with the eyes of the dead-alive men he had reslain. Drool plashed his torn chest.

Then did the mage break his own spell in his self-confidence:

"Life is well-lived here, Kimon of Koneria, and for a man such as you—life is better here than in the shallow world outside!"

The mists faded from Kimon's brain as if dissipated by the morning sun. Again his eyes, clear and blazing, stared up the steps at the black-robed man. "Life? Call you this foul illusion LIFE? Call you the world of living men SHALLOW? Nay, sorcerer, 'tis your necromancy that is shallow! Your world is DEATH, and I shall see that you join the other dead things in it."

"Kimon," Reh said, rolling up his sleeves, "you are a pain in the neck."

One foot Kimon set upon the steps, and then Reh extended his arms. Wrists like clean-picked skeletons emerged from his sleeves. Blue light flickered and danced at his fingertips. In the instant that he stiffened his arms, pointing his talons at the barbarian to fry him, Kimon flung up his own hand to aim the ring. He shouted, three ringing times, "I DEFY YOU!"

Lightning leapt from Reh's hands. Down at Kimon it crackled, in sizzling streams the colour of cobalt. It flashed before his face so that he winced and closed his eyes against the searing glare. But he felt nothing; nothing save the power coursing down his arm from the ring, shaking him as a cobweb shakes in the wind.

He opened his eyes. All around him shimmered the blue-sizzling lightning, but it was checked, held at bay by the power of the ring. With a wild roar he hurled himself up the stairs, holding the ring before him and swinging up Goreater. His war cry shattered the air: "WHEEEEE-EEE!"

"The ring!" Reh shouted, and fear tinged his voice. "You have the lyon ring of Sprag! How did you—it negates my magic! No—get back—NO—"

Reh of Atramentos died screaming and waving his skeletal arms as Goreater bit through his skull and forehead and nose and mouth and neck and was covered to the hilt with his gore. Kimon left the body where it lay and bounded back down the stairs, slipping in blood and falling the last sixteen feet. He waded again through that noisome river of gore with its islands of headless corpses. Down the dim corridor he rushed and up another, leaving scarlet prints, until he found the huge brassbound door Kohl had described.

Goreater's first bite split it in twain, and Kimon jerked back the hinged half. He descended into darkness.

And descended. He counted to ten, his limit, and folded down a finger and began again, and then repeated the action, and still again. There were, naturally, nine-and-forty steps; seven times seven. Yet somehow the air remained fresh, though growing steadily cooler and damper. He stalked forward into gloom, wishing that he had brought a torch. But ahead was a glow as of a glim.

He rounded a corner into light, so sudden and bright that he squinted and put up a hand before his eyes. Then Kimon swung up his dripping sword, for he saw the man.

He wore arms and armour, the nosepiece of his helmet making his face a sinister mask of pallor. First the man raised a hand in command to halt, spreading two fingers, but he carried it quickly to his mouth as he sneezed. No wonder, Kimon thought, reflecting on the universal dampness of dungeons. Throughout history, inferior workmanship had made dungeons damp and dank.

He raised his gory glaive and started forward.

The man's hands sprang to his rusty buckle, and let his belt and sword clang to the dewy floor. "Thank the gods! You'b cobe to rescue me! Dake her, dake the Brincess Sabell! And free be too, *blease!* Guard, he called be—Me—and unwilling warder hab I been, bearing food and water and wine and thunderbucket for the poor girl here." He stepped back, sniffing, and extended his arm to hold out a ring bearing one huge gey. Key.

Sheathing his sword, Kimon took it. By the light of a hundred flickering torches, fed by some sorcerous well of air in this chthonian place, he looked into the barred cell.

She was beautiful. Her hair was liquid gold, flowing down over her shoulders, capping arms round and snowy-white. Her bosom was to the liking of any man: big, alive, with her excited breathing. Her shift, he saw with more interest than compassion, was badly torn and far too thin for the chill damp of her prison. Her eyes swept his tall figure. She sneezed.

Shaded by their lids, Kimon's eyes were still on the girl as he bent to the lock. Her nose was slightly red—but who was looking at her nose?

"A man named Kohl sent me hither, Princess. He said you alone knew the whereabouts of some treasure—which

I of course promised to him. I came here only as a hero
to rescue you from that villainous Reh. But I have found
my treasure in you. . . ."

She nodded without speaking. Her eyes were bright
on the lock.

"Ah!" she breathed, as the key clicked and he swung
open the grille. She stood within, lovely and fair, and
Kimon thought that never had he seen such a comely
woman, despite the red nose. He held out a hand; she extended hers. He went to her, seized her arms, and drew
her strongly to him so that his lips could drink the nectar
of hers. Her eyelids lowered as she raised her face.

"Now, Kandentos," she said, and then her mouth was
beneath Kimon's.

The ceiling fell on his head. She twisted from his
grasp as he fell forward onto the cell's floor. He was
stunned but not unconscious, having been hit only by the
edge of Kandentos' blade. Kimon rolled over and looked
up before wasting the time necessary to rise; that had
saved his life more than once. He saw the guard Kandentos
doffing his helmet and dropping it onto the sword he had
used on Kimon's head. Without the noseguard, the gaoler's
nose was enlarged and red. Kimon's growl rumbled up
in his throat.

The girl fairly flung Kandentos from the cell. She
whirled to slam the door and twist the key and hurl it
ringing along the corridor. Clutching Kandentos' arm, she
turned to Kimon, her lip curling. Kimon wondered at the
fresh crimson smears on her shift.

"You idiot barbarian!" she snapped nasally. "You
male chauvinist HAWG! You dumb atavist! Look at you

—a big murdering brute; all over blood and gore—and your *odour!*" She turned again to her former gaoler, who was industriously wiping Kimon's blood from the bodice of her shift. "Kandentos," she sniffed, *"thinks!"*

And they kissed.

"Come, Kandentos my love, let's go find the treasure." She kissed him again. "Umm! YOU're not all blood and gore—ouch! Be careful of my arms, that meathead apeman bruised them!" Clutching Kandentos' arm, swinging her hips against his, she glanced back at Kimon.

"Br-r-r-a-a-a-ak!"

Watching them hurry up the corridor to the steps, Kimon sneezed.

endit

Glossary of terms

phrase	source	meaning
Atrabilos	atrabilious	black
Atramentos	atramentous	black
basalt	igneous rock	black
black basalt	" "	a redundancy
chthonian	underworldly	black
Kohl	a cosmetic	black
Minaceos	minaceous	black
Minatoa	minatory	black
moonless		black
dark; darkling		black
Nigressa	nigrescent	black
nigrescent	"	black
Sabell	heraldic: sable	black
sombre, shadowy,	etc etc etc	black
umbrageous	shadowy	black
Kandentos	candent	white
Reh		initials of a much-copied writer of note; dead he is, but his work lives on to line the pockets of others.

positively the end

GALLEGHER PLUS
HENRY KUTTNER

GALLEGHER PEERED DIMLY THROUGH THE WINDOW AT THE place where his backyard should have been and felt his stomach dropping queasily into that ridiculous, unlikely hole gaping there in the earth. It was big, that hole. And deep. Almost deep enough to hold Gallegher's slightly colossal hangover.

But not quite. Gallegher wondered if he should look at the calendar, and then decided against it. He had a feeling that several thousand years had passed since the beginning of the binge. Even for a man with his thirst and capacity, it had been one hell of a toot.

"Toot," Gallegher mourned, crawling toward the couch and collapsing on it. "Binge is far more expressive.

Toot makes me think of fire engines and boat whistles, and I've got those in my head, anyway—all sounding off at once." He reached up weakly for the siphon of the liquor organ, hesitated, and communed briefly with his stomach.

GALLEGHER: Just a short one, maybe?

STOMACH: Careful, there!

GALLEGHER: A hair of the dog—

STOMACH: O-O-O-OH!

GALLEGHER: Don't do that! I need a drink. My backyard's disappeared.

STOMACH: I wish I could.

At this point the door opened and a robot entered, wheels, cogs, and gadgets moving rapidly under its transparent skin plate. Gallegher took one look and closed his eyes, sweating.

"Get out of here," he snarled. "I curse the day I ever made you. I hate your revolving guts."

"You have no appreciation of beauty," said the robot in a hurt voice. "Here. I've brought you some beer."

"Hm-m-m!" Gallegher took the plastibulb from the robot's hand and drank thirstily. The cool catnip taste tingled refreshingly against the back of his throat. "A-ah," he said, sitting up. "That's a little better. Not much, but—"

"How about a thiamin shot?"

"I've become allergic to the stuff," Gallegher told his robot morosely. "I'm cursed with thirst. Hm-m-m!" He looked at the liquor organ. "Maybe—"

"There's a policeman to see you."

"A what?"

"A policeman. He's been hanging around for quite a while."

"Oh," Gallegher said. He stared into a corner by an open window. "What's that?"

It looked like a machine of some curious sort. Gallegher eyed it with puzzled interest and a touch of amazement. No doubt he had built the damned thing. That was the only way the erratic scientist ever worked. He'd had no technical training, but, for some weird reason, his subconscious mind was gifted with a touch of genius. Conscious, Gallegher was normal enough, though erratic and often drunk. But when his demon subconscious took over, anything was liable to happen. It was in one of these sprees that he had built this robot, spending weeks thereafter trying to figure out the creature's basic purpose. As it turned out, the purpose wasn't an especially useful one, but Gallegher kept the robot around, despite its maddening habit of hunting up mirrors and posturing vainly before them, admiring its metallic innards.

"I've done it again," Gallegher thought. Aloud he said, "More beer, stupid. Quick."

As the robot went out, Gallegher uncoiled his lanky body and wandered across to the machine, examining it curiously. It was not in operation. Through the open window extended some pale, limber cables as thick as his thumb; they dangled a foot or so over the edge of the pit where the backyard should have been. They ended in—Hm-m-m! Gallegher pulled one up and peered at it. They ended in metal-rimmed holes, and were hollow. Odd.

The machine's over-all length was approximately two yards, and it looked like an animated junk heap. Gallegher had a habit of using makeshifts. If he couldn't find the right sort of connection, he'd snatch the nearest suit-able object—a buttonhook, perhaps, or a coat hanger—and use that. Which meant that a qualitative analysis of an already-assembled machine was none too easy. What, for example, was that fibroid duck doing wrapped around with wires and nestling contentedly on an antique waffle iron?

"This time I've gone crazy," Gallegher pondered. "However, I'm not in trouble as usual. Where's that beer?"

The robot was before a mirror, staring fascinated at his middle. "Beer? Oh, right here. I paused to steal an admiring little glance at me."

Gallegher favored the robot with a foul oath, but took the plastibulb. He blinked at the gadget by the win-dow, his long, bony face twisted in a puzzled scowl. The end product—

The ropy hollow tubes emerged from a big feed box that had once been a wastebasket. It was sealed shut now, though a gooseneck led from it into a tiny convertible dynamo, or its equivalent. "No," Gallegher thought. "Dynamos are big, aren't they? Oh, I wish I'd had a tech-nical training. How can I figure this out, anyway?"

There was more, much more, including a square gray metal locker—Gallegher, momentarily off the beam, tried to estimate its contents in cubic feet. He made it four hundred eighty-six, which was obviously wrong, since the box was only eighteen inches by eighteen inches by eight-een inches.

The door of the locker was closed; Gallegher let it pass temporarily and continued his futile investigation.

There were more puzzling gadgets. At the very end was a wheel, its rim grooved, diameter four inches.

"End product—what? Hey, Narcissus."

"My name is not Narcissus," the robot said reprovingly

"It's enough to have to look at you, without trying to remember your name," Gallegher snarled. "Machines shouldn't have names, anyhow. Come over here."

"Well?"

"What *is* this?"

"A machine," the robot said, "but by no means as lovely as I."

"I hope it's more useful. What does it do?"

"It eats dirt."

"Oh. That explains the hole in the backyard."

"There *is* no backyard," the robot pointed out accurately.

"There is."

"A backyard," said the robot, quoting in a confused manner from Thomas Wolfe, "is not only backyard but the negation of backyard. It is the meeting in Space of backyard and no backyard. A backyard is finite and unextended dirt, a fact determined by its own denial."

"Do you know what you're talking about?" Gallegher demanded, honestly anxious to find out.

"Yes."

"I see. Well, try and keep the dirt out of your conversation. I want to know why I built this machine."

"Why ask me? I've been turned off for days—weeks, in fact."

"Oh, yeah. I remember. You were posing before the mirror and wouldn't let me shave that morning."

"It was a matter of artistic integrity. The planes of my functional face are far more coherent and dramatic than yours."

"Listen, Narcissus," Gallegher said, keeping a grip on himself. "I'm trying to find out something. Can the planes of your blasted functional brain follow that?"

"Certainly," Narcissus said coldly. "I can't help you. You turned me on again this morning and fell into a drunken slumber. The machine was already finished. It wasn't in operation. I cleaned house and kindly brought you beer when you woke up with your usual hang-over."

"Then kindly bring me some more and shut up."

"What about the policeman?"

"Oh, I forgot him. Uh . . . I'd better see the guy. I suppose."

Narcissus retreated on softly padding feet. Gallegher shivered, went to the window, and looked out at that incredible hole. Why? How? He ransacked his brain. No use, of course. His subconscious had the answer, but it was locked up there firmly. At any rate, he wouldn't have built the machine without some good reason. Or would he? His subconscious possessed a peculiar, distorted sort of logic. Narcissus had originally been intended as a super beer-can opener.

A muscular young man in a dapper uniform came in after the robot. "Mr. Gallegher?" he asked.

"Yeah."

"Mr. Galloway Gallegher?"

"The answer's still 'yeah.' What can I do for you?"

"You can accept this summons," said the cop. He gave Gallegher a folded paper.

The maze of intricate legal phraseology made little sense to Gallegher. "Who's Dell Hopper?" he asked. "I never heard of him."

"It's not my pie," the officer grunted. "I've served the summons; that's as far as I go."

He went out. Gallegher peered at the paper. It told him little.

Finally, for lack of something better to do, he televised an attorney, got in touch with the bureau of legal records, and found the name of Hopper's lawyer, a man named Trench. A corporation lawyer at that. Trench had a battery of secretaries to take calls, but by dint of threats, curses and pleas Gallegher got through to the great man himself.

On the telescreen Trench showed as a gray, thin, dry man with a clipped moustache. His voice was file-sharp.

"Mr. Gallegher? Yes?"

"Look," Gallegher said, "I just had a summons served on me."

"Ah, you have it, then. Good."

"What do you mean, good? I haven't the least idea what this is all about."

"Indeed," Trench said skeptically. "Perhaps I can refresh your memory. My client, who is soft-hearted, is not prosecuting you for slander, threat of bodily harm, or assault and battery. He just wants his money back—or else value received."

Gallegher closed his eyes and shuddered. "H-he does? I . . . ah . . . did I slander him?"

"You called him," said Trench, referring to a bulky file, "a duck-footed cockroach, a foul-smelling Neanderthaler, and either a dirty cow or a dirty *cao*. Both are terms of opprobium. You also kicked him."

"When was this?" Gallegher whispered.

"Three days ago."

"And—you mentioned money?"

"A thousand credits, which he paid you on account."

"On account of what?"

"A commission you were to undertake for him. I was not acquainted with the exact details. In any case, you not only failed to fulfill the commission, but you refused to return the money."

"Oh. Who is Hopper, anyway?"

"Hopper Enterprises, Inc.—Dell Hopper, entrepreneur and impresario. However, I think you know all this. I will see you in court, Mr. Gallegher. And, if you'll forgive me, I'm rather busy. I have a case to prosecute today, and I rather think the defendant will get a long prison sentence."

"What did he do?" Gallegher asked weakly.

"Simple case of assault and battery," Trench said. "Good-by."

His face faded from the screen. Gallegher clapped a hand to his forehead and screamed for beer. He went to his desk, sucking at the plastibulb with its built-in refrigerant, and thoughtfully examined his mail. Nothing there. No clue.

A thousand credits—He had no recollection of getting them. But the cash book might show—

It did. Under dates of several weeks back, it said:

Rec'd D.H.—com.—on acc't—c1,000
Rec'd J.W.—com.—on acc't—c1,500
Rec'd Fatty—com.—on acc't—c800

Thirty-three hundred credits! And the bank book had no record of that sum. It showed merely a withdrawal of seven hundred credits, leaving about fifteen still on hand.

Gallegher moaned and searched his desk again. Under a blotter he found an envelope he had previously over-looked. It contained stock certificates—both common and preferred—for something called Devices Unlimited. A covering letter acknowledged receipt of four thousand credits, in return for which payment stock had been issued to Mr. Galloway Gallegher, as ordered—

"Murder," Gallegher said. He gulped beer, his mind swirling. Trouble was piling up in triplicate. D. H.—Dell Hopper—had paid him a thousand credits to do something or other. Someone whose initials were J. W. had given his fifteen hundred credits for a similar purpose. And Fatty, the cheapskate, had paid only eight hundred credits on account.

Why?

Only Gallegher's mad subconscious knew. That

brainy personality had deftly arranged the deals, collected the dough, depleted Gallegher's personal bank account—cleaning it out—and bought stock in Devices Unlimited. Ha!

Gallegher used the televisor again. Presently he beamed his broker.

"Arnie?"

"Hi, Gallegher," Arnie said, looking up at the teleplate over his desk. "What's up?"

"I am. At the end of a rope. Listen, did I buy some stock lately?"

"Sure. In Devices—DU."

"Then I want to sell it. I need the dough, quick."

"Wait a minute." Arnie pressed buttons. Current quotations were flashing across his wall, Gallegher knew.

"Well?"

"No soap. The bottom's dropped out. Four asked, nothing bid."

"What did I buy at?"

"Twenty."

Gallegher emitted the howl of a wounded wolf. "*Twenty?* And you let me do that?"

"I tried to argue you out of it," Arnie said wearily. "Told you the stock was skidding. There's a delay in a construction deal or something—not sure just what. But you said you had inside info. What could I do?"

"You could have beaten my brains out," Gallegher said. "Well, never mind. It's too late now. Have I got any other stock?"

"A hundred shares of Martian Bonanza."

"Quoted at?"

"You could realize twenty-five credits on the whole lot."

"What are the bugles blowin' for?" Gallegher murmured.

"Huh?"

"I'm dreadin' what I've got to watch—"

"I know," Arnie said happily. "Danny Deever."

"Yeah," Gallegher agreed. "Danny Deever. Sing it at my funeral, chum." He broke the beam.

Why, in the name of everything holy and unholy, had he bought that DU stock?

What had he promised Dell Hopper of Hopper Enterprises?

Who were J. W. (fifteen hundred credits) and Fatty (eight hundred credits)?

Why was there a hole in place of his backyard?

What and why was that confounded machine his subconscious had built?

He pressed the directory button on the televisor, spun the dial till he located Hopper Enterprises, and called that number.

"I want to see Mr. Hopper."

"Your name?"

"Gallegher."

"Call our lawyer, Mr. Trench."

"I did," Gallegher said. "Listen—"

"Mr. Hopper is busy."

"Tell him," Gallegher said wildly, "that I've got what he wanted."

That did it. Hopper focused in, a buffalo of a man with a mane of gray hair, intolerant jet-black eyes, and a beak of a nose. He thrust his jutting jaw toward the screen and bellowed, "Gallegher? For two pins I'd—" He changed his tune abruptly. "You called Trench, eh? I thought that'd do the trick. You know I can send you to prison, don't you?"

"Well, maybe—"

"Maybe nothing! Do you think I come personally to see every crackpot inventor who does some work for me? If I hadn't been told over and over that you were the best man in your field, I'd have slapped an injunction on you days ago!"

Inventor?

"The fact is," Gallegher began mildly, "I've been ill—"

"In a pig's eye," Hopper said coarsely. "You were drunk as a lord. I don't pay men for drinking. Did you forget those thousand credits were only part payment— with nine thousand more to come?"

"Why . . . why, n-no. Uh . . . nine thousand?"

"Plus a bonus for quick work. You still get the bonus, luckily. It's only been a couple of weeks. But it's lucky for you you got the thing finished. I've got options on a couple of factories already. *And* scouts looking out for good locations, all over the country. Is it practical for small sets, Gallegher? We'll make our steady money from them, not from the big audiences."

"*Tchwuk*," Gallegher said. "Uh—"

"Got it there? I'm coming right down to see it."

"Wait! Maybe you'd better let me add a few touches—"

"All I want is the idea," Hopper said. "If that's satisfactory, the rest is easy. I'll call Trench and have him quash that summons. See you soon."

He blanked out.

Gallegher screamed for beer. "And a razor," he added, as Narcissus padded out of the room. "I want to cut my throat."

"Why?" the robot asked.

"Just to amuse you, why else? Get that beer."

Narcissus brought a plastibulb. "I don't understand why you're so upset," he remarked. "Why don't you lose yourself in rapturous contemplation of my beauty?"

"Better the razor," Gallegher said glumly. "Far better. Three clients, two of whom I can't remember at all, commissioning me to do jobs I can't remember, either. Ha!"

Narcissus ruminated. "Try induction," he suggested. "That machine—"

"Well, when you get a commission, you usually drink yourself into such a state that your subconscious takes over and does the job. Then you sober up. Apparently that's what happened this time. You made the machine, didn't you?"

"Sure," Gallegher said, "but for which client? I don't even know what it does."

"You could try it and find out."

"Oh. So I could. I'm stupid this morning."

"You're always stupid," Narcissus said. "And very ugly, too. The more I contemplate my own perfect loveliness, the more pity I feel for humans."

"Oh, shut up," Gallegher snapped, feeling the uselessness of trying to argue with a robot. He went over to the enigmatic machine and studied it once more. Nothing clicked in his mind.

There was a switch, and he flipped it. The machine started to sing "St. James Infirmary."

"—to see my sweetie there

She was lying on a marble sla-a-ab—"

"I see it all," Gallegher said in a fit of wild frustration. "Somebody asked me to invent a phonograph."

"Wait," Narcissus pointed out. "Look at the window."

"The window. Sure. What about it? *Wh*—" Gallegher hung over the sill, gasping. His knees felt unhinged and weak. Still, he might have expected something like this.

The group of tubes emerging from the machine were rather incredibly telescopic. They had stretched down to the bottom of the pit, a full thirty feet, and were sweeping around in erratic circles like grazing vacuum cleaners. They moved so fast Gallegher couldn't see them except as blurs. It was like watching the head of a Medusa who had contracted St. Vitus' Dance and transmitted the ailment to her snakes.

"Look at them whiz," Narcissus said contemplatively, leaning heavily on Gallegher. "I guess that's what made the hole. They eat dirt."

"Yeah," the scientist agreed, drawing back. "I wonder why. Dirt—Hm-m-m. Raw material." He peered at the machine, which was wailing:

"—can search the wide world over

And never find another sweet man like me."

"Electrical connections," Gallegher mused, cocking an inquisitive eye. "The raw dirt goes in that one-time wastebasket. Then what? Electronic bombardment? Protons, neutrons, positrons—I *wish* I knew what those words meant," he ended plaintively. "If only I'd had a college education!"

"A positron is—"

"Don't tell me," Gallegher pleaded. "I'll only have semantic difficulties. I know what a positron is, all right, only I don't identify it with that name. All I know is the intensional meaning. Which can't be expressed in words, anyhow."

"The extensional meaning can, though," Narcissus pointed out.

"Not with me. As Humpty Dumpty said, the question is: Which is to be master? And with me it's the word. The damn things scare me. I simply don't get their extensional meanings."

"That's silly," said the robot. "Positron has a perfectly clear denotation."

"To you. All it means to me is a gang of little boys with fishtails and green whiskers. That's why I never can figure out what my subconscious has been up to. I have to use symbolic logic, and the symbols . . . ah, shut up," Gallegher growled. "Why should I argue about semantics with you, anyhow?"

"You started it," Narcissus said.

Gallegher glared at the robot and then went back to the cryptic machine. It was still eating dirt and playing "St. James Infirmary."

"Why should it sing that, I wonder?"

"You usually sing it when you're drunk, don't you? Preferably in a barroom."

"That solves nothing," Gallegher said shortly. He explored the machine. It was in smooth, rapid operation, emitting a certain amount of heat, and something was smoking. Gallegher found a lubricating valve, seized an oil can, and squirted. The smoke vanished, as well as a faint smell of burning.

"Nothing comes out," Gallegher said, after a long pause of baffled consideration.

"There?" The robot pointed.

Gallegher examined the grooved wheel that was turning rapidly. Just above it was a small circular aperture in the smooth hide of a cylindrical tube. Nothing seemed to be coming out of that hole, however.

"Turn the switch off," Gallegher said. Narcissus obeyed. The valve snapped shut and the grooved wheel stopped turning. Other activity ceased instantly. The music died. The tentacles stretched out the window stopped whirling and shortened to their normal inactive length.

"Well, there's apparently no end product," Gallegher remarked. "It eats dirt and digests it completely. Ridiculous."

"Is it?"

"Sure. Dirt's got elements in it. Oxygen, nitrogen—there's granite under New York, so there's aluminum, sodium, silicon—lots of things. No sort of physical or chemical change could explain this."

"You mean something ought to come out of the machine?"

"Yes," Gallegher said. "In a word, exactly. I'd feel a lot better if something did. Even mud."

"Music comes out of it," Narcissus pointed out. "If you can truthfully call that squalling music."

"By no stretch of my imagination can I bring myself to consider that loathsome thought," the scientist denied firmly. "I'll admit my subconscious is slightly nuts. But it's got logic, in a mad sort of way. It wouldn't build a machine to convert dirt into music, even if such a thing's possible."

"But it doesn't do anything else, does it?"

"No. Ah. Hm-m-m. I wonder what Hopper asked me to make for him. He kept talking about factories and audiences."

"He'll be here soon," Narcissus said. "Ask him."

Gallegher didn't bother to reply. He thought of demanding more beer, rejected the idea, and instead used the liquor organ to mix himself a pick-me-up of several liqueurs. After that he went and sat on a generator which bore the conspicuous label of Monstro. Apparently dissatisfied, he changed his seat to a smaller generator named Bubbles.

Gallegher always thought better atop Bubbles.

The pick-me-up had oiled his brain, fuzzy with alcohol fumes. A machine without an end product—dirt vanishing into nothingness. Hm-m-m. Matter cannot disappear like a rabbit popping into a magician's hat. It's got to go somewhere. Energy?

Apparently not. The machine didn't manufacture energy. The cords and sockets showed that, on the contrary, it made use of electric power to operate.

And so—

What?

Try it from another angle. Gallegher's subsconscious, Gallegher Plus, had built the device for some logical reason. The reason was supplied by his profit of thirty-three hundred credits. He'd been paid that sum, by three different people, to make—maybe—three different things.

Which of them fitted the machine?

Look at it as an equation. Call clients a, b, and c. Call the purpose of the machine—not the machine itself, of course—x. Then a (or) b (or) c equals x.

Not quite. The term a wouldn't represent Dell Hopper; it would symbolize what he wanted. And what he wanted must necessarily and logically be the purpose of the machine.

Or the mysterious J. W., or the equally mysterious Fatty.

Well, Fatty was a shade less enigmatic. Gallegher had a clue, for what it was worth. If J. W. was represented by b, Fatty would be c plus adipose tissue. Call adipose tissue t, and what did you get?

Thirsty.

Gallegher had more beer, distracting Narcissus from his posturing before the mirror. He drummed his heels against Bubbles, scowling, a lock of dark hair falling lankly over his eyes.

Prison?

Uh! No, there must be some other answer, somewhere. The DU stock, for example. Why had Gallegher Plus bought four thousand credits' worth of the stuff when it was on the skids?

If he could find the answer to that, it might help. For Gallegher Plus did nothing without purpose. What was Devices Unlimited, anyway?

He tried the televisor Who's Who in Manhattan. Luckily Devices was corporated within the State and had business offices here. A full-page ad flipped into view.

DEVICES UNLIMITED
WE DO EVERYTHING!
RED 5-1400-M

Well, Gallegher had the firm's 'visor number, which was something. As he began to call RED, a buzzer murmured, and Narcissus turned petulantly from the mirror and went off to answer the door. He returned in a moment with the bisonlike Mr. Hopper.

"Sorry to be so long," Hopper rumbled. "My chauffeur went through a light, and a cop stopped us. I had to bawl the very devil out of him."

"The chauffeur?"

"The cop. Now where's the stuff?"

Gallegher licked his lips. Had Gallegher Plus actually kicked this mountainous guy in the pants? It was not a thought to dwell upon.

He pointed toward the window. "There." Was he right? Had Hopper ordered a machine that ate dirt?

The big man's eyes widened in surprise. He gave Gallegher a swift, wondering look, and then moved toward the device, inspecting it from all angles. He glanced out the window, but didn't seem much interested in what he saw there. Instead, he turned back to Gallegher with a puzzled scowl.

"You mean this? A totally new principle, is it? But then it must be."

No clue there. Gallegher tried a feeble smile. Hopper just looked at him.

"All right," he said. "What's the practical application?"

Gallegher groped wildly. "I'd better show you," he said at last, crossing the lab and flipping the switch. Instantly the machine started to sing "St. James Infirmary." The tentacles lengthened and began to eat dirt. The hole in the cylinder opened. The grooved wheel began to revolve.

Hopper waited.

After a time he said, "Well?"

"You—don't like it?"

"How should I know? I don't even know what it does. Isn't there any screen?"

"Sure," Gallegher said, completely at a loss. "It's inside that cylinder."

"In—*what?*" Hopper's shaggy brows drew down over his jet-black eyes. "*Inside that cylinder?*"

"Uh-huh."

"For—" Hopper seemed to be choking. "What good is it there? Without X-ray eyes, anyhow?"

"Should it have X-ray eyes?" Gallegher muttered, dizzy with bafflement. "You wanted a screen with X-ray eyes?"

"You're still drunk!" Hopper snarled. "Or else you're crazy!"

"Wait a minute. Maybe I've made a mistake—"

"A mistake!"

"Tell me one thing. Just what did you ask me to do?"

Hopper took three deep breaths. In a cold, precise voice he said, "I asked you if you could devise a method of projecting three-dimensional images that could be viewed from any angle, front, back or side, without distortion. You said yes. I paid you a thousand credits on account. I've taken options on a couple of factories so I could begin manufacturing without delay. I've had scouts out looking for likely theaters. I'm planning a campaign for selling the attachments to home televisors. And now, Mr. Gallegher, I'm going out and see my attorney and tell him to put the screws on."

He went out, snorting. The robot gently closed the door, came back, and, without being asked, hurried after beer. Gallegher waved it away.

"I'll use the organ," he moaned, mixing himself a stiff one. "Turn that blasted machine off, Narcissus. I haven't the strength."

"Well, you've found out one thing," the robot said encouragingly. "You didn't build the device for Hopper."

"True. True. I made it for . . . ah . . . either J. W. or Fatty. How can I find out who they are?"

"You need a rest," the robot said. "Why not simply relax and listen to my lovely melodious voice? I'll read to you."

"It's not melodious," Gallegher said automatically and absently. "It squeaks like a rusty hinge."

"To your ears. *My* senses are different. To me, your voice is the croaking of an asthmatic frog. You can't see me as I do, any more than you can hear me as I hear myself. Which is just as well. You'd swoon with ecstasy."

"Narcissus," Gallegher said patiently. "I'm trying to think. Will you kindly shut your metallic trap?"

"My name isn't Narcissus," said the robot. "It's Joe."

"Then I'm changing it. Let's see. I was checking up on DU. What was that number?"

"Red five fourteen hundred M."

"Oh, yeah." Gallegher used the televisor. A secretary was willing but unable to give much useful information.

Devices Unlimited was the name of a holding company, of a sort. It had connections all over the world. When a client wanted a job done, DU, through its agents, got in touch with the right person and finagled the deal. The trick was that DU supplied the money, financing operations and working on a percentage basis. It sounded fantastically intricate, and Gallegher was left in the dark.

"Any record of my name in your files? Oh—Well, can you tell me who J. W. is?"

"J. W.? I'm sorry, sir. I'll need the full name—"

"I don't have it. And this is important." Gallegher argued. At last he got his way. The only DU man whose initials were J. W. was someone named Jackson Wardell, who was on Callisto at the moment.

"How long has he been there?"

"He was born there," said the secretary unhelpfully. "He's never been to Earth in his life. I'm sure Mr. Wardell can't be your man."

Gallegher agreed. There was no use asking for Fatty,

he decided, and broke the beam with a faint sigh. Well, what now?

The visor shrilled. On the screen appeared the face of a plump-cheeked, bald, pudgy man who was frowning worriedly. He broke into a relieved chuckle at sight of the scientist.

"Oh, there you are, Mr. Gallegher," he said. "I've been trying to reach you for an hour. Something's wrong with the beam. My goodness, I thought I'd certainly hear from you before this!"

Gallegher's heart stumbled. *Fatty*—of course!

Thank God, the luck was beginning to turn! Fatty—eight hundred credits. On account. On account of what? The machine? Was it the solution to Fatty's problem, or to J. W.'s? Gallegher prayed with brief fervency that Fatty had requested a device that ate dirt and sang "St. James Infirmary."

The image blurred and flickered, with a faint crackling. Fatty said hurriedly, "Something's wrong with the line. But—did you do it, Mr. Gallegher? Did you find a method.

"Sure," Gallegher said. If he could lead the man on, gain some hint of what he had ordered—

"Oh, wonderful! DU's been calling me for days. I've been putting them off, but they won't wait forever. Cuff's bearing down hard, and I can't get around that old statute—"

The screen went dead.

Gallegher almost bit off his tongue in impotent fury.

Hastily he closed the circuit and began striding around the lab, his nerves tense with expectation. In a second the visor would ring. Fatty would call back. Naturally. And this time the first question Gallegher would ask would be, "Who are you?"

Time passed.

Gallegher groaned and checked back, asking the operator to trace the call.

"I'm sorry, sir. It was made from a dial visor. We cannot trace calls made from a dial visor."

Ten minutes later Gallegher stopped cursing, seized his hat from its perch atop an iron dog that had once decorated a lawn, and whirled to the door. "I'm going out," he snapped to Narcissus. "Keep an eye on that machine."

"All right. One eye." The robot agreed. "I'll need the other to watch my beautiful insides. Why don't you find out who Cuff is?"

"What?"

"Cuff. Fatty mentioned somebody by that name. He said he was bearing down hard—"

"Check! He did, at that. And—what was it?—he said he couldn't get around an old statue—"

"Statute. It means a law."

"I know what statute means," Gallegher growled. "I'm not exactly a driveling idiot. Not yet, anyhow. Cuff, eh? I'll try the visor again."

There were six Cuffs listed. Gallagher eliminated half of them by gender. He crossed off Cuff-Linx Mfg. Co., which left two—Max and Fredk. He televised Frederick, getting a pop-eyed, scrawny youth who was obviously not yet old enough to vote. Gallegher gave the lad a murderous glare of frustration and flipped the switch, leaving Frederick to spend the next half-hour wondering who had called him, grimaced like a demon, and blanked out without a word.

But Max Cuff remained, and that, certainly, was the man. Gallegher felt sure of it when Max Cuff's butler transferred the call to a downtown office, where a receptionist said that Mr. Cuff was spending the afternoon at the Uplift Social Club.

"That so? Say, who is Cuff, anyhow?"

"I beg your pardon?"

"What's his noise? His business, I mean?"

"Mr. Cuff has no business," the girl said frigidly. "He's an alderman."

That was interesting. Gallegher looked for his hat, found it on his head, and took leave of the robot, who did not trouble to answer. "If Fatty calls up again," the scientist commanded, "get his name. See? And keep your eye on that machine, just in case it starts having mutations or something."

That seemed to tie up all the loose ends. Gallegher let himself out of the house. A cool autumn wind was blowing, scattering crisp leaves from the overhead parkways. A few taxiplanes drifted past, but Gallegher hailed a street cab; he wanted to see where he was going. Somehow he felt that a telecall to Max Cuff would produce little of value. The man would require deft handling, especially since he was "bearing down hard."

"Where to, bud?"

"Uplift Social Club. Know where it is?"

"Nope," said the driver, "but I can find out." He used his teledirectory on the dashboard. "Downtown. 'Way down."

"O.K.," Gallegher told the man, and dropped back on the cushions, brooding darkly. Why was everybody so elusive? His clients weren't usually ghosts. But Fatty remained vague and nameless—a face, that was all, and one Gallegher hadn't recognized. Who J. W. was anyone might guess. Only Dell Hopper had put in an appearance, and Gallegher wished he hadn't. The summons rustled in his pocket.

"What I need," Gallegher soliloquized, "is a drink. That was the whole trouble. I didn't stay drunk. Not long enough, anyhow. Oh, damn."

Presently the taxi stopped at what had once been a glass-brick mansion, now grimy and forlorn-looking. Gallegher got out, paid the driver, and went up the ramp. A small placard said Uplift Social Club. Since there was no buzzer, he opened the door and went in.

Instantly his nostrils twitched like the muzzle of a war horse scenting cordite. There was drinking going on. With the instinct of a homing pigeon, Gallegher went directly to the bar, set up against one wall of a huge room filled with chairs, tables, and people. A sad-looking man with a derby was playing a pin-ball machine in a corner. He looked up as Gallegher approached, lurched into his path, and murmured, "Looking for somebody?"

"Yeah," Gallegher said. "Max Cuff. They told me he was here."

"Not now," said the sad man. "What do you want with him?"

"It's about Fatty," Gallegher hazarded.

Cold eyes regarded him. "Who?"

"You wouldn't know him. But Max would."

"Max want to see you?"

"Sure."

"Well," the man said doubtfully, "he's down at the Three-Star on a pub-crawl. When he starts that—"

"The Three-Star? Where is it?"

"Fourteenth near Broad."

"Thanks," Gallegher said. He went out, with a longing look at the bar. Not now—not yet. There was business to attend to first.

The Three-Star was a gin mill, with dirty pictures on the walls. They moved in a stereoscopic and mildly appalling manner. Gallegher, after a thoughtful examination, looked the customers over. There weren't many. A huge man at one end of the bar attracted his attention because of the gardenia in his lapel and the flashy diamond on his ring finger.

Gallegher went toward him. "Mr. Cuff?"

"Right," said the big man, turning slowly on the barstool like Jupiter revolving on its axis. He eyed Gallegher, librating slightly. "Who're you?"

"I'm—"

"Never mind," said Cuff, winking. "Never give your right name after you've pulled a job. So you're on the lam, eh?"

"What?"

"I can spot 'em as far away as I can see 'em. You . . . you . . . hey!" Cuff said, bending forward and sniffing. "You been *drinking!*"

"Drinking," Gallegher said bitterly. "It's an understatement."

"Then have a drink with me," the big man invited. "I'm up to E now. Egg flip. Tim!" he roared. " 'Nother egg flip for my pal here! Step it up! And get busy with F."

Gallegher slid onto the stool beside Cuff and watched his companion speculatively. The alderman seemed a little tight.

"Yes," Cuff said, "alphabetical drinking's the only way to do it. You start with A—absinthe—and then work along, brandy, cointreau, daiquiri, egg flip—"

"Then what?"

"F, of course," Cuff said, mildly surprised. "Flip. Here's yours. Good lubrication!"

They drank. "Listen," Gallegher said, "I want to see you about Fatty."

"Who's he?"

"Fatty," Gallegher explained, winking significantly. "You know. You've been bearing down lately. The statute. You know."

"Oh! *Him!*" Cuff suddenly roared with Gargantuan laughter. "Fatty, huh? That's good. That's very good. Fatty's a good name for him, all right."

"Not much like his own, is it?" Gallegher said cunningly.

"Not a bit. Fatty!"

"Does he spell his name with an e or an i?"

"Both," Cuff said. "Tim, where's the flip? Oh, you got it ready, huh? Well, good lubrication, pal."

Gallegher finished his egg flip and went to work on the flip, which was identical except for the name. What now?

"About Fatty," he hazarded.

"Yeah?"

"How's everything going?"

"I never answer questions," Cuff said, abruptly sobering. He looked sharply at Gallegher. "You one of the boys? I don't know you."

"Pittsburgh. They told me to come to the club when I got in town."

"That doesn't make sense," Cuff said. "Oh, well, it doesn't matter. I just cleaned up some loose ends, and I'm celebrating. Through with your flip? Tim! Gin!"

They had gin for G, a horse's neck for H, and a eye-opener for I. "Now a Jazzbo," Cuff said with satisfaction. "This is the only bar in town that has a drink beginning with J. After that I have to start skipping. I dunno any K drinks."

"Kirchwasser," Gallegher said absently.

"K—huh? What's that?" Cuff bellowed at the bartender. "Tim! You got any kirchwasser?"

"Nope," said the man. "We don't carry it, Alderman."

"Then we'll find somebody who does. You're a smart guy, pal. Come along with me. I *need* you."

Gallegher went obediently. Since Cuff didn't want to talk about Fatty, it behooved him to win the alderman's confidence. And the best way to do that was to drink with him. Unfortunately an alphabetical pub-crawl, with its fantastic mixtures, proved none too easy. Gallegher already had a hangover. And Cuff's thirst was insatiable.

"L? What's L?"

"Lachrymae Christi. Or Liebfraumilch."

"Oh, boy!"

It was a relief to get back to a Martini. After the Orange Blossom Gallegher began to feel dizzy. For R he suggested root beer, but Cuff would have none of that.

"Well, rice wine."

"Yeah. Rice—hey! We missed N! We gotta start over now from A!"

Gallegher dissuaded the alderman with some trouble, and succeeded only after fascinating Cuff with the exotic name ng ga po. They worked on, through sazeracs, tailspins, undergrounds, and vodka. W meant whiskey.

"X?"

They looked at each other through alcoholic fogs. Gallegher shrugged and stared around. How had they got into this swanky, well-furnished private clubroom, he wondered. It wasn't the Uplift, that was certain. Oh, well—

"X?" Cuff insisted. "Don't fail me now, pal."

"Extra whiskey," Gallegher said brilliantly.

"That's it. Only two left. Y and . . . and—what comes after Y?"

"Fatty. Remember?"

"Ol' Fatty Smith," Cuff said, beginning to laugh immoderately. At least, it sounded like Smith. "Fatty just suits him."

"What's his first name?" Gallegher asked.

"Who?"

"Fatty."

"Never heard of him," Cuff said, and chuckled. A page boy came over and touched the alderman's arm.

"Someone to see you, sir. They're waiting outside."

"Right. Back in a minute, pal. Everybody always knows where to find me—'specially here. Don't go 'way. There's still Y and . . . and . . . and the other one."

He vanished. Gallegher put down his untasted drink, stood up, swaying slightly, and headed for the lounge. A televisor booth there caught his eye, and, on impulse, he went in and vised his lab.

"Drunk again," said Narcissus, as the robot's face appeared on the screen.

"You said it," Gallegher agreed. "I'm . . . urp . . . high as a kite. But I got a clue, anyway."

"I'd advise you to get a police escort," the robot said. "Some thugs broke in looking for you, right after you left."

"S-s-some what? Say that again."

"Three thugs," Narcissus repeated patiently. "The leader was a thin, tall man in a checkered suit with yellow hair and a gold front tooth. The others—"

"I don't want a description," Gallegher snarled. "Just tell me what happened?"

"Well, that's all. They wanted to kidnap you. Then they tried to steal the machine. I chased them out. For a robot, I'm pretty tough."

"Did they hurt the machine?"

"What about me?" Narcissus demanded plaintively.

"I'm much more important than that gadget. Have you no curiosity about my wounds?"

"No," Gallegher said. "Have you some?"

"Of course not. But you could have demonstrated some slight curiosity—"

"*Did they hurt that machine?*"

"I didn't let them get near it," the robot said. "And the hell with you."

"I'll ring you back," Gallegher said. "Right now I need black coffee."

He beamed off, stood up, and wavered out of the booth. Max Cuff was coming toward him. There were three men following the alderman.

One of them stopped short, his jaw dropping. "Cripes!" he said. "That's the guy, boss. That's Gallegher. Is he the one you been drinking with?"

Gallegher tried to focus his eyes. The man swam into clarity. He was a tall, thin chap in a checkered suit, and he had yellow hair and a gold front tooth.

"Conk him," Cuff said. "Quick, before he yells. And before anybody else comes in here. Gallegher, huh? Smart guy, huh?"

Gallegher saw something coming at his head, and tried to leap back into the visor booth like a snail retreating into its shell. He failed. Spinning flashes of glaring light dazzled him.

He was conked.

The trouble with this social culture, Gallegher thought dreamily, was that it was suffering both from over-

growth and calcification of the exoderm. A civilization may
be likened to a flowerbed. Each individual plant stands for
a component part of the culture. Growth is progress.
Technology, that long-frustrated daffodil, had had B_1 con-
centrate poured on its roots, the result of wars that forced
its growth through sheer necessity. But no world is satisfactory unless the parts are equal to the whole.

The daffodil shaded another plant that developed
parasitic tendencies. It stopped using its roots. It wound
itself around the daffodil, climbing up on its stem and
stalks and leaves, and that strangling liana was religion, politics, economics, culture—outmoded forms that changed
too slowly, outstripped by the blazing comet of the
sciences, riding high in the unlocked skies of this new era.
Long ago writers had theorized that in the future—their
future—the sociological pattern would be different. In the
day of rocketships such illogical *mores* as watered stock,
dirty politics, and gangsters would not exist. But those
theorists had not seen clearly enough. They thought of
rocketships as vehicles of the far distant future.

Armstrong and Aldrin landed on the moon before
automobiles stopped using carburetors.

The great warfare of the early twentieth century gave
a violent impetus to technology, and that growth continued. Unfortunately most of the business of living was
based on such matters as man-hours and monetary fixed
standards. The only parallel was the day of the great
bubbles—the Mississippi Bubble and its brothers. It was,
finally, a time of chaos, reorganization, shifting precar-
iously from old standards to new, and a seesaw bouncing

vigorously from one extreme to the other. The legal profession had become so complicated that batteries of experts needed Pedersen Calculators and the brain machines of Mechanistra to marshal their farfetched arguments, which went wildly into uncharted realms of symbolic logic and—eventually—pure nonsense. A murderer would get off scot-free provided he didn't sign a confession. And even if he did, there were ways of discrediting solid, legal proof. Precedents were shibboleths. In that maze of madness, administrators turned to historical solidities—legal precedents—and these were often twisted against them.

Thus it went, all down the line. Later sociology would catch up with technology. It hadn't, just yet. Economic gambling had reached a pitch never before attained in the history of the world. Geniuses were needed to straighten out the mess. Mutations eventually provided such geniuses, by natural compensation; but a long time was to pass until that satisfactory conclusion had been reached. The man with the best chance for survival, Gallegher had realized by now, was one with a good deal of adaptability and a first-class all-around stock of practical and impractical knowledge, versed in practically everything. In short, in matters vegetable, animal or mineral—

Gallegher opened his eyes. There was little to see, chiefly because, as he immediately discovered, he was slumped face down at a table. With an effort Gallegher sat up. He was unbound, and in a dimly lighted attic that seemed to be a storeroom; it was littered with broken-down junk. A fluorescent burned faintly on the ceiling. There was a door, but the man with the gold tooth was standing before it. Across the table sat Max Cuff, carefully pouring whiskey into a glass.

"I want some," Gallegher said feebly.

Cuff looked at him. "Awake, huh? Sorry Blazer socked you so hard."

"Oh, well. I might have passed out anyway. Those alphabetical pub-crawls are really something."

"Heigh-ho," Cuff said, pushing the glass toward Gallegher and filling another for himself. "That's the way it goes. It was smart of you to stick with me—the one place the boys wouldn't think of looking."

"I'm naturally clever," Gallegher said modestly. The whiskey revived him. But his mind still felt foggy. "Your . . . uh . . . associates, by which I mean lousy thugs, tried to kidnap me earlier, didn't they?"

"Uh-huh. You weren't in. That robot of yours—"

"He's a beaut."

"Yeah. Look, Blazer told me about the machine you had set up. I'd hate to have Smith get his hands on it."

Smith—Fatty. Hm-m-m. The jigsaw was dislocated again. Gallegher sighed.

If he played the cards close to his chest—

"Smith hasn't seen it yet."

"I know that," Cuff said. "We've been tapping his visor beam. One of our spies found out he'd told DU he had a man working on the job—you know? Only he didn't mention the man's name. All we could do was shadow Smith and tap his visor till he got in touch with you. After that—well, we caught the conversation. You told Smith you'd got the gadget."

"Well?"

"We cut in on the beam, fast, and Blazer and the boys went down to see you. I told you I didn't want Smith to keep that contract."

"You never mentioned a contract," Gallegher said.

"Don't play dumb. Smith told 'em, up at DU, that he'd laid the whole case before you."

Maybe Smith had. Only Gallegher had been drunk at the time, and it was Gallegher Plus who had listened, storing the information securely in the subconscious.

"So?"

Cuff burped. He pushed his glass away suddenly. "I'll see you later. I'm tight, damn it. Can't think straight. But—I don't want Smith to get that machine. Your robot won't let us get near it. You'll get in touch with him by visor and send him off somewhere, so the boys can pick up your gadget. Say yes or no. If it's no, I'll be back."

"No," Gallegher said. "On account of you'd kill me anyway, to stop me from building another machine for Smith."

Cuff's lids drew down slowly over his eyes. He sat motionless, seemingly asleep, for a time. Then he looked at Gallegher blankly and stood up.

"I'll see you later, then." He rubbed a hand across his forehead; his voice was a little thick. "Blazer, keep the lug here."

The man with the gold tooth came forward. "You O.K.?"

"Yeah. I can't think—" Cuff grimaced. "Turkish bath. That's what I need." He went toward the door, pulling Blazer with him. Gallegher saw the alderman's lips move. He read a few words.

"—drunk enough . . . vise that robot . . . try it—"

Then Cuff went out. Blazer came back, sat opposite Gallegher, and shoved the bottle toward him. "Might as well take it easy," he suggested. "Have another; you need it."

Gallegher thought: Smart guys. They figure if I get stinko, I'll do what they want. Well—

There was another angle. When Gallegher was thoroughly under the influence of alcohol, his subconscious took over. And Gallegher Plus was a scientific genius—mad, but good.

Gallegher Plus might be able to figure a way out of this.

"That's it," Blazer said, watching the liquor vanish. "Have another. Max is a good egg. He wouldn't put the bee on you. He just can't stand people helixing up his plans."

"What plans?"

"Like with Smith," Blazer explained.

"I see." Gallegher's limbs were tingling. Pretty soon he should be sufficiently saturated with alcohol to unleash his subconscious. He kept drinking.

Perhaps he tried too hard. Usually Gallegher mixed his liquor judiciously. This time, the factors of the equation added up to a depressing zero. He saw the surface of the table moving slowly toward his nose, felt a mild, rather pleasant bump, and began to snore. Blazer got up and shook him.

"One half so precious as the stuff they sell," Gallegher said thickly. "High-piping Pehlevi, with wine, wine, wine, wine. *Red* wine."

"Wine he wants," Blazer said. "The guy's a human blotter." He shook Gallegher again, but there was no response. Blazer grunted, and his footsteps sounded, growing fainter.

Gallegher heard the door close. He tried to sit up, slid off the chair, and banged his head agonizingly against a table leg.

It was more effective than cold water. Wavering, Gallegher crawled to his feet. The attic room was empty except for himself and other jetsam. He walked with abnormal carefulness to the door and tried it. Locked. Reinforced with steel, at that.

"Fine stuff," Gallegher murmured. "The one time I need my subconscious, it stays buried. How the devil can I get out of here?"

There was no way. The room had no windows, and the door was firm. Gallegher floated toward the piles of junk. An old sofa. A box of scraps. Pillows. A rolled carpet. Junk.

Gallegher found a length of wire, a bit of mica, a twisted spiral of plastic, once part of a mobile statuette and some other trivia. He put them together. The result was a thing vaguely resembling a gun, though it had some resemblance to an egg beater. It looked as weird as a Martian's doodling.

After that, Gallegher returned to the chair and sat down, trying, by sheer will power, to sober up. He didn't succeed too well. When he heard footsteps returning, his mind was still fuzzy.

The door opened. Blazer came in, with a swift, wary glance at Gallegher, who had hidden the gadget under the table.

"Back, are you? I thought it might be Max."

"He'll be along, too," Blazer said. "How d'you feel?"

"Woozy. I could use another drink. I've finished this bottle." Gallegher had finished it. He had poured it down a rat hole.

Blazer locked the door and came forward as Gallegher stood up. The scientist missed his balance, lurched forward, and Blazer hesitated. Gallegher brought out the crazy egg-beater gun and snapped it up to eye level, squinting along its barrel at Blazer's face.

The thug went for something, either his gun or his sap. But the eerie contrivance Gallegher had leveled at him worried Blazer. His motion was arrested abruptly. He was wondering what menace confronted him. In another second he would act, one way or another—perhaps continuing that arrested smooth motion toward his belt.

Gallegher did not wait. Blazer's stare was on the gadget. With utter disregard for the Queensbury Rules, Gallegher kicked his opponent below the belt. As Blazer folded up, Gallegher followed his advantage by hurling himself headlong on the thug and bearing him down in a wild, octopuslike thrashing of lanky limbs. Blazer kept trying to reach his weapon, but that first foul blow had handicapped him.

Gallegher was still too drunk to co-ordinate properly.

He compromised by crawling atop his enemy and beating the man repeatedly on the solar plexus. Such tactics proved effective. After a time, Gallegher was able to wrench the sap from Blazer's grasp and lay it firmly along the thug's temple.

That was that.

With a glance at the gadget, Gallegher arose, wondering what Blazer had thought it was. A death-ray projector, perhaps. Gallegher grinned faintly. He found the door key in his unconscious victim's pocket, let himself out of the attic, and warily descended a stairway. So far, so good.

A reputation for scientific achievements has its advantages. It had, at least, served the purpose of distracting Blazer's attention from the obvious.

What now?

The house was a three-story, empty structure near the Battery. Gallegher escaped through a window. He did not pause till he was in an airtaxi, speeding uptown. There, breathing deeply, he flipped the wind filter and let the cool night breeze cool his perspiring cheeks. A full moon rode high in the black autumn sky. Below, through the earth-view transparent panel, he could see the brilliant ribbons of streets, with slashing bright diagonals marking the upper level speedways.

Smith. Fatty Smith. Connected with DU, somehow—

He paid off the pilot and stepped out on a rooftop landing in the White Way district. There were televisor booths here, and Gallegher called his lab. The robot answered.

"Narcissus—"

"Joe," the robot corrected. "And you've been drinking some more. Why don't you sober up?"

"Shut up and listen. What's been happening?"

"Not much."

"Those thugs. Did they come back?"

"No," Narcissus said, "but some officers came to arrest you. Remember that summons they served you with today? You should have appeared in court at 5 P.M."

Summons. Oh, yeah. Dell Hopper—one thousand credits.

"Are they there now?"

"No. I said you'd taken a powder."

"Why?" asked Gallegher.

"So they wouldn't hang around. Now you can come home whenever you like—if you take reasonable precautions."

"Such as what?"

"That's your problem," Narcissus said. "Get a false beard. I've done my share."

Gallegher said, "All right, make a lot of black coffee. Any other calls?"

"One from Washington. A commander in the space police unit. He didn't give his name."

"Space police! Are they after me, too? What did he want?"

"You," the robot said. "Good-by. You interrupted a lovely song I was singing to myself."

"Make that coffee," Gallegher ordered as the image faded. He stepped out of the booth and stood for a moment, considering, while he stared blankly at the towers of Manhattan rising around him, with their irregular patterns of lighted windows, square, oval, circular, crescent, or star-shaped.

A call from Washington.

Hopper cracking down.

Max Cuff and his thugs.

Fatty Smith.

Smith was the best bet. He tried the visor again, calling DU.

"Sorry, we have closed for the day."

"This is important," Gallegher insisted. "I need some information. I've got to get in touch with a man—"

"I'm sorry."

"S-m-i-t-h," Gallegher spelled. "Just look him up in the file or something, won't you? Or do you want me to cut my throat while you watch?" He fumbled in his pocket.

"If you will call tomorrow—"

"That'll be too late. Can't you just look it up for me? Please. Double please."

"Sorry."

"I'm a stockholder in DU," Gallegher snarled. "I warn you, my girl!"

"A . . . oh. Well, it's irregular, but—S-m-i-t-h? One moment. The first name is what?"

"I don't know. Give me all the Smiths."

The girl disappeared and came back with a file box labeled SMI. "Oh, dear," she said, riffling through the cards. "There must be several hundred Smiths."

Gallegher groaned. "I want a fat one," he said wildly.

"There's no way of checking on that, I suppose."

The secretary's lips tightened. "Oh, a rib. I see. Good *night!*" She broke the connection.

Gallegher sat staring at the screen. Several hundred Smiths. Not so good. In fact, definitely bad.

Wait a minute. He had bought DU stock when it was on the skids. Why? He must have expected a rising market. But the stock had continued to fall, according to Arnie.

There might be a lead there.

He reached Arnie at the broker's home and was insistent. "Break the date. This won't take you long. Just find out for me why DU's on the skids. Call me back at my lab. Or I'll break your neck. And make it fast! Get that dope, understand?"

Arnie said he would. Gallegher drank black coffee at a counter stand, went home warily by taxi, and let himself into his house. He double-locked the door behind him. Narcissus was dancing before the big mirror in the lab.

"Any calls?" Gallegher said.

"No. Nothing's happened. Look at this graceful *pas.*"

"Later. If anybody tries to get in, call me. I'll hide till you can get rid of 'em." Gallegher squeezed his eyes shut. "Is the coffee ready?"

"Black and strong. In the kitchen."

The scientist went into the bathroom instead, stripped, cold-showered, and took a brief irradiation. Feeling less woozy, he returned to the lab with a gigantic cup full of steaming coffee. He perched on Bubbles and gulped the liquid.

"You look like Rodin's Thinker," Narcissus remarked. "I'll get you a robe. Your ungainly body offends my aesthetic feelings."

Gallegher didn't hear. He donned the robe, since his sweating skin felt unpleasantly cool, but continued to drink the coffee and stare into space.

"Narcissus. More of this."

Equation: a (or) b (or) c equals x. He had been trying to find the value of a, b, or c. Maybe that was the wrong way. He hadn't located J.W. at all. Smith remained a phantom. And Dell Hopper (one thousand credits) had been of no assistance.

It might be better to find the value of x. That blasted machine must have some purpose. Granted, it ate dirt. But matter cannot be destroyed; it can be changed into other forms.

Dirt went into the machine; nothing came out.

Nothing visible.

Free energy?

That was invisible, but could be detected with instruments.

Voltmeter, ammeter—gold leaf—

Gallegher turned the machine on again briefly. Its singing was dangerously loud, but no one rang the door buzzer, and after a minute or two Gallegher snapped the switch back to OFF. He had learned nothing.

Arnie called. The broker had secured the information Gallegher wanted.

" 'Twasn't easy. I had to pull some wires. But I found out why DU stock's been dropping."

"Thank heaven for that! Spill it."

"DU's a sort of exchange, you know. They farm out jobs. This one—it's a big office building to be constructed in downtown Manhattan. Only the contractor hasn't been able to start yet. There's a lot of dough tied up in the deal, and there's a whispering campaign that's hurt the DU stock."

"Keep talking."

Arnie went on. "I got all the info. I could, in case. There were two firms bidding on the job."

"Who?"

"Ajax, and somebody named—"

"Not Smith?"

"That's it," Arnie said. "Thaddeus Smith. S-m-e-i-t-h, he spells it."

There was a long pause. "S-m-e-i-t-h," Gallegher repeated at last. "So that's why the girl at DU couldn't . . . eh? Oh, nothing. I ought to have guessed it." Sure. When he'd asked Cuff whether Fatty spelled his name with an e or an i, the alderman had said both. Smeith. Ha!

"Smeith got the contract," Arnie continued. "He underbid Ajax. However, Ajax has political pull. They got some alderman to clamp down and apply an old statute that put the kibosh on Smeith. He can't do a thing."

"Why not?"

"Because," Arnie said, "the law won't permit him to block Manhattan traffic. It's a question of air rights. Smeith's client—or DU's client, rather—bought the property lately, but air rights over it had been leased for a ninety-nine-year period to Transworld Strato. The stratoliners have their hangar just beyond that property, and you know they're not gyros. They need a straightaway course

for a bit before they can angle up. Well, their right of
way runs right over the property. Their lease is good. For
ninety-nine years they've got the right to use the air over
that land, above and over fifty feet above ground level."

Gallegher squinted thoughtfully. "How could Smeith
expect to put up a building there, then?"

"The new owner possesses the property from fifty
feet above soil down to the center of the earth. Savvy? A
big eighty-story building—most of it underground. It's
been done before, but not against political pull. If Smeith
fails to fulfill his contract, the job goes to Ajax—and Ajax
is hand-in-glove with that alderman."

"Yeah. Max Cuff," Gallegher said. "I've met the lug.
Still—what's this statute you mentioned?"

"An old one, pretty much obsolete, but still on the
books. It's legal. I checked. You can't interfere with downtown traffic, or upset the stagger system of transport."

"Well?"

"If you dig a hole for an eighty-story building,"
Arnie said, "you get a lot of dirt and rock. How can you
haul it away without upsetting traffic? I didn't try to figure
out how many tons have to be removed."

"I see," Gallegher said softly.

"So there it is, on a platinum platter. Smeith took the
contract. Now he's stymied. He can't get rid of the dirt
he'll be excavating, and pretty soon Ajax will take over
and wangle a permit to truck out the material."

"How—if Smeith can't?"

"Remember the alderman? Well, a few weeks ago
some of the streets downtown were blocked off, for re-
pairs. Traffic was rerouted—right by that building site.

It's been siphoned off there, and it's so crowded that dirt trucks would tangle up the whole business. Of course it's temporary"—Arnie laughed shortly—"temporary until Smeith is forced out. Then the traffic will be rerouted again, and Ajax can wangle their permit."

"Oh." Gallegher looked over his shoulder at the machine. "There may be a way—"

The door buzzer rang. Narcissus made a gesture of inquiry. Gallegher said, "Do me another favor, Arnie. I want to get Smeith down here to my lab, quick."

"All right, vise him."

"His visor's tapped. I don't dare. Can you hop over and bring him here, right away?"

Arnie sighed. "I certainly earn my commissions the hard way. But O.K."

He faded. Gallegher listened to the door buzzer, frowned and nodded to the robot. "See who it is. I doubt it Cuff would try anything now, but—well, find out. I'll be in this closet."

He stood in the dark, waiting, straining his ears, and wondering. Smeith—he had solved Smeith's problem. The machine ate dirt. The only effective way to get rid of earth without running the risk of a nitrogen explosion.

Eight hundred credits, on account, for a device or a method that would eliminate enough earth—safely—to provide space for an underground office building, a structure that had to be mostly subterranean because of prior-leased air rights.

Fair enough.

Only—*where did that dirt go?*

Narcissus returned and opened the closet door. "It's

a Commander John Wall. He vised from Washington earlier tonight. I told you, remember?"

"John Wall?"

J.W., fifteen hundred credits! The third client!

"Let him in," Gallegher ordered breathlessly. "Quick! Is he alone?"

"Yes."

"Then step it up!"

Narcissus padded off, to return with a gray-haired, stocky figure in the uniform of the space police. Wall grinned briefly at Gallegher, and then his keen eyes shot toward the machine by the window.

"That it?"

Gallegher said, "Hello, Commander. I . . . I'm pretty sure that's it. But I want to discuss some details with you first."

Wall frowned. "Money? You can't hold up the government. Or am I misjudging you? Fifty thousand credits should hold you for a while." His face cleared. "You have fifteen hundred already; I'm prepared to write you a check as soon as you've completed a satisfactory demonstration."

"Fifty thou—" Gallegher took a deep breath. "No, it isn't that, of course. I merely want to make certain that I've filled the terms of our agreement. I want to be sure I've met every specification." If he could only learn what Wall had requested! If he, too, had wanted a machine that ate dirt—

It was a farfetched hope, an impossible coincidence, but Gallegher had to find out. He waved the commander to a chair.

"But we discussed the problem in full detail—"

"A double-check," Gallegher said smoothly. "Narcissus, get the commander a drink."

"Thanks, no."

"Coffee?"

"I'd be obliged. Well, then—as I told you some weeks ago, we needed a spaceship control—a manual that would meet the requirements of elasticity and tensile strength."

"Oh-oh," Gallegher thought.

Wall leaned forward, his eyes brightening. "A spaceship is necessarily big and complicated. Some manual controls are required. But they cannot move in a straight line; construction necessitates that such controls must turn sharp corners, follow an erratic and eccentric path from *here* to *here*."

"Well—"

"Thus," Wall said, "you want to turn on a water faucet in a house two blocks away. And you want to do it while you're here, in your laboratory. How?"

"String. Wire. Rope."

"Which could wind around corners as . . . say . . . a rigid rod could not. However, Mr. Gallegher, let me repeat my statement of two weeks ago. *That faucet is hard to turn*. And it must be turned often, hundreds of times a day when a ship is in free space. Our toughest wire cables have proved unsatisfactory. The stress and strain snap them. When a cable is *bent*, and when it is also *straight* —you see?"

Gallegher nodded. "Sure. You can break wire by bending it back and forth often enough."

"That is the problem we asked you to solve. You said it could be done. Now—have you done it? And how."

A manual control that could turn corners and withstand repeated stresses. Gallegher eyed the machine. Nitrogen—a thought was moving in the back of his mind, but he could not quite capture it.

The buzzer rang. "Smeith," Gallegher thought, and nodded to Narcissus. The robot vanished.

He returned with four men at his heels. Two of them were uniformed officers. The others were, respectively, Smeith and Dell Hopper.

Hopper was smiling savagely. "Hello, Gallegher," he said. "We've been waiting. We weren't fast enough when this man"—he nodded toward Commander Wall—"came in, but we waited for a second chance."

Smeith, his plump face puzzled, said, "Mr. Gallegher, what is this? I rang your buzzer, and then these men surrounded me—"

"It's O.K.," Gallegher said. "You're on top, at least. Look out that window."

Smeith obeyed. He popped back in again, beaming. "That hole—"

"Right. I didn't cart the dirt away, either. I'll give you a demonstration presently."

"You will in jail," Hopper said acidly. "I warned you, Gallegher, that I'm not a man to play around with. I gave you a thousand credits to do a job for me, and you neither did the job nor returned the money."

Commander Wall was staring, his coffee cup, forgotten, balanced in one hand. An officer moved forward and took Gallegher's arm.

"Wait a minute," Wall began, but Smeith was quicker.

"I think I owe Mr. Gallegher some credits," he said,

snatching out a wallet. "I've not much more than a thousand on me, but you can take a check for the balance, I suppose. If this—gentleman—wants cash, there should be a thousand here."

Gallegher gulped.

Smeith nodded at him encouragingly. "You did my job for me, you know. I can begin construction—and excavation—tomorrow. Without bothering to get a trucking permit, either."

Hopper's teeth showed. "The devil with the money! I'm going to teach this man a lesson! My time is worth plenty, and he's completely upset my schedule. Options, scouts—I've gone ahead on the assumption that he could do what I paid him for, and now he blandly thinks he can wiggle out. Well, Mr. Gallegher, you can't. You failed to observe that summons you were handed today, which makes you legally liable to certain penalties—and you're going to suffer them, Gammit!"

Smeith looked around. "But—I'll stand good for Mr. Gallegher. I'll reimburse—"

"No!" Hopper snapped.

"The man says no," Gallegher murmured. "It's just my heart's blood he wants. Malevolent little devil, isn't he?"

"You drunken idiot!" Hopper snarled. "Take him to the jail, officers. Now!"

"Don't worry, Mr. Gallegher," Smeith encouraged. "I'll have you out in no time. I can pull a few wires myself."

Gallegher's jaw dropped. He breathed hoarsely, in an asthmatic fashion, as he stared at Smeith, who drew back.

"Wires," Gallegher whispered. "And a . . . a stereo-

scopic screen that can be viewed from any angle. You said
—wires!"

"Take him away," Hopper ordered brusquely.

Gallegher tried to wrench away from the officers
holding him. "Wait a minute! One minute! I've got the
answer now. It *must* be the answer. Hopper, I've done
what you wanted—and you, too, Commander. Let me
go."

Hopper sneered and jerked his thumb toward the
door. Narcissus walked forward, cat-footed. "Shall I break
their heads, chief?" he inquired gently. "I like blood. It's a
primary color."

Commander Wall put down his coffee cup and rose,
his voice sounding crisp and metallic. "All right, officers.
Let Mr. Gallegher go."

"Don't do it," Hopper insisted. "Who are you, anyway? A space captain!"

Wall's weathered cheeks darkened. He brought out a
badge in a small leather case. "Commander Wall," he said.
"Administrative Space Commission. You"—he pointed to
Narcissus—"I'm deputizing you as a government agent,
pro tem. If these officers don't release Mr. Gallegher in
five seconds, go on and break their heads."

But that was unnecessary. The Space Commission was
big. It had the government behind it, and local officials
were, by comparison, small potatoes. The officers hastily
released Gallegher and tried to look as though they'd
never touched him.

Hopper seemed ready to explode. "By what right do
you interfere with justice, Commander?" he demanded.

"Right of priority. The government needs a device

Mr. Gallegher has made for us. He deserves a hearing, at least."

"He does *not!*"

Wall eyed Hopper coldly. "I think he said, a few moments ago, that he had fulfilled your commission also."

"With that?" The big shot pointed to the machine. "Does that look like a stereoscopic screen?"

Gallegher said, "Get me an ultraviolet, Narcissus. Fluorescent." He went to the device, praying that his guess was right. But it had to be. There was no other possible answer. Extract nitrogen from dirt or rock, extract all gaseous content, and you have inert matter.

Gallagher touched the switch. The machine started to sing "St. James Infirmary." Commander Wall looked startled and slightly less sympathetic. Hopper snorted. Smeith ran to the window and ecstatically watched the long tentacles eat dirt, swirling madly in the moonlit pit below.

"The lamp, Narcissus."

It was already hooked up on an extension cord. Gallegher moved it slowly about the machine. Presently he had reached the grooved wheel at the extreme end, farthest from the window.

Something fluoresced.

It fluoresced blue—emerging from the little valve in the metal cylinder, winding about the grooved wheel, and piling in coils on the laboratory floor. Gallegher touched the switch; as the machine stopped, the valve snapped shut, cutting off the blue, cryptic thing that emerged from the cylinder. Gallegher picked up the coil. As he moved the light away, it vanished. He brought the lamp closer— it reappeared.

"Here you are, Commander," he said. "Try it."

Wall squinted at the fluorescence. "Tensile strength?"

"Plenty," Gallegher said. "It has to be. Nonorganic, mineral content of solid earth, compacted and compressed into wire. Sure, it's got tensile strength. Only you couldn't support a ton weight with it."

Wall nodded. "Of course not. It would cut through steel like a thread through butter. Fine, Mr. Gallegher. We'll have to make tests—"

"Go ahead. It'll stand up. You can run this wire around corners all you want, from one end of a spaceship to another, and it'll never snap under stress. It's too thin. It won't—it can't—be strained unevenly, because it's too thin. A wire cable couldn't do it. You needed flexibility that wouldn't cancel tensile strength. The only possible answer was a thin, tough wire."

The commander grinned. That was enough.

"We'll have the routine tests," he said. "Need any money now, though? We'll advance anything you need, within reason—say up to ten thousand."

Hopper pushed forward. "I never ordered wire, Gallegher. So you haven't fulfilled my commission."

Gallegher didn't answer. He was adjusting his lamp. The wire changed from blue to yellow fluorescence, and then to red.

"This is your screen, wise guy," Gallegher said. "See the pretty colors?"

"Naturally I see them! I'm not blind. But—"

"Different colors, depending on how many angstroms I use. Thus. Red. Blue. Red again. Yellow. And when I turn off the lamp—"

The wire Wall still held became invisible.

Hopper closed his mouth with a snap. He leaned forward, cocking his head to one side.

Gallegher said, "The wire's got the same refractive index as air. I made it that way, on purpose." He had the grace to blush slightly. Oh, well—he could buy Gallegher Plus a drink later.

"On purpose?"

"You wanted a stereoscopic screen which could be viewed from any angle without optical distortion. And in color—that goes without saying, these days. Well, here it is."

Hopper breathed hard.

Gallegher beamed at him, "Take a box frame and string each square with this wire. Make a mesh screen. Do that on all four sides. String enough wires inside of the box. You have, in effect, an invisible cube, made of wire. All right. Use ultraviolet to project your film or your television, and you have patterns of fluorescence, depending on the angstrom strength patterns. In other words—a picture. A colored picture. A three-dimensional picture, because it's projected onto an invisible cube. And, finally, one that can be viewed from any angle without distortion, because it does more than give an optical illusion of stereoscopic vision—it's actually a three-dimensional picture. Catch?"

Hopper said feebly, "Yes. I understand. You . . . why didn't you tell me this before?"

Gallegher changed the subject in haste. "I'd like some police protection, Commander Wall. A crook named Max Cuff has been trying to get his hooks on this machine. His thugs kidnaped me this afternoon, and—"

"Interfering with government business, eh?" Wall

said grimly. "I know these jackpot politicians. Max Cuff won't trouble you any more—if I may use the visor?"

Smeith beamed at the prospect of Cuff getting it in the neck. Gallegher caught his eye. There was a pleasant, jovial gleam in it, and somehow, it reminded Gallegher to offer his guests drinks. Even the commander accepted this time, turning from his finished visor call to take the glass Narcissus handed him.

"Your laboratory will be under guard," he told Gallegher. "So you'll have no further trouble."

He drank, stood up, and shook Gallegher's hand. "I must make my report. Good luck, and many thanks. We'll call you tomorrow."

He went out, after the two officers. Hopper, gulping his cocktail, said, "I ought to apologize. But it's all water under the bridge, eh, old man?"

"Yeah," Gallegher said. "You owe me some money."

"Trench will mail you the check. And . . . uh . . . and—" His voice died away.

"Something?"

"N-nothing," Hopper said, putting down his glass and turning green. "A little fresh air . . . urp!"

The door slammed behind him. Gallegher and Smeith eyed each other curiously.

"Odd," Smeith said.

"A visitation from heaven, maybe," Gallegher surmised. "The mills of the gods—"

"I see Hopper's gone," Narcissus said, appearing with fresh drinks.

"Yeah. Why?"

"I thought he would. I gave him a Mickey Finn," the

robot explained. "He never looked at me once. I'm not exactly vain, but a man so insensitive to beauty deserves a lesson. Now don't disturb me. I'm going into the kitchen and practice dancing, and you can get your own liquor out of the organ. You may come and watch if you like."

Narcissus spun out of the lab, his innards racing. Gallegher sighed.

"That's the way it goes," he said.

"What?"

"Oh, I dunno. Everything. I get, for example, orders for three entirely different things, and I get drunk and make a gadget that answers all three problems. My sub-conscious does things the easy way. Unfortunately, it's the hard way for me—after I sober up."

"Then why sober up?" Smeith asked cogently. "How does that liquor organ work?"

Gallegher demonstrated. "I feel lousy," he confided. "What I need is either a week's sleep, or else—"

"What?"

"A drink. Here's how. You know—one item still worries me."

"What, again?"

"The question of why that machine sings 'St. James Infirmary' when it's operating."

"It's a good song," Smeith said.

"Sure, but my subconscious works logically. Crazy logic, I'll admit. Nevertheless—"

"Here's how," Smeith said.

Gallegher relaxed. He was beginning to feel like himself again. A warm, rosy glow. There was money in the bank. The police had been called off. Max Cuff was, no doubt, suffering for his sins. And a heavy thumping announced that Narcissus was dancing in the kitchen.

It was past midnight when Gallegher choked on a drink and said, "Now I remember!"

"Swmpmf," Smeith said, startled. "Whatzat?"

"I feel like singing."

"So what?"

"Well, I feel like singing 'St. James Infirmary'."

"Go right ahead," Smeith invited.

"But not alone," Gallegher amplified. "I always like to sing that when I get tight, but I figure it sounds best as a duet. Only I was alone when I was working on that machine."

"Ah?"

"I must have built in a recording play-back," Gallegher said, lost in a vast wonder at the mad resources and curious deviations of Gallegher Plus. "My goodness. A machine that performs four operations at once. It eats dirt, turns out a spaceship manual control, makes a stereoscopic nondistorting projection screen, and sings a duet with me. How strange it all seems."

Smeith considered. "You're a genius."

"That, of course. Hm-m-m." Gallegher got up, turned on the machine, and returned to perch atop Bubbles. Smeith, fascinated by the spectacle, went to hang on the window sill and watch the flashing tentacles eat dirt. Invisible wire spun out along the grooved wheel. The calm of the night was shattered by the more or less melodious tones of the "St. James Infirmary."

Above the lugubrious voice of the machine rose a

deeper bass, passionately exhorting someone unnamed to search the wild world over.

"But you'll never find
Another sweet ma-a-ahn like me."

Gallegher Plus was singing, too.

ABOUT THE COMPILER

JOE HALDEMAN WAS BORN IN OKLAHOMA CITY, OKLA-HOMA. In college he majored in physics and astronomy and took his degree at the University of Maryland. Upon graduation he was drafted into the Army and served in Vietnam.

Mr. Haldeman began his writing career after his discharge. Science fiction is his specialty and he has written numerous short stories and a novel, as well as lecturing on the subject. In addition his semi-autobiographical novel *War Year* was published recently.